To dog lovers —
Buddy dog lovers —

Alice Twiggs Vantrease

Oliver

The Hootchie Cootchie Pickler

and

Other Southern Tales

2015

Disclaimer

This is a work of fiction. Names, characters, places, and incidents are the product of the author's imagination. Thus, any resemblance to actual persons, living or dead, business establishments, events, or locales is entirely coincidental.

ISBN: 1505331552

Additional copies may be ordered from CreateSpace.com or Amazon.com.

Acknowledgments

These short stories and memoirs might never have been completed without the encouragement of Christopher Scott and other fellow writers during meetings of Savannah Authors . Thank you all! You listened to me read many times and steered me in the right direction -- for that I am eternally grateful.

Appreciation is due my favorite Yankee friends in Savannah, Cameron Spencer and Susan Johnson, for their editing assistance and for bolstering my belief in this project whenever my faith in it wavered. Their persistence in pointing out odd words and activities peculiar to the South, which are familiar to me but were foreign to them, hopefully make these stories more understandable given the context and time in which they occur.

My grandmother said, "Be nice to your girlfriends, because you're going to need them when you are old." She was right. I must also thank my good friends Betsy Thurmond Keller, Jeanette Baynham Eckard, Carol Douglas Goodwin, Tina Joers Roberts, Keith Claussen, Sally Speicher Booth, May Swenson Mahoney, and my cosmic sister Judy Margaret Greer. Thank you for your help with this project.

This one is for my children:

Sarah Elizabeth Marks

and

John Mulford Marks, Jr.

I am so proud of you.

The Hootchie Cootchie Pickler

and Other Southern Tales

Table of Contents

x

The Corn Field Flasher

When I was young, no one gave a second thought to letting young girls ride horses through the countryside unaccompanied by an adult. It couldn't be done today; there are too many weirdoes lurking about, and some are dangerous.

My friend and I loved horseback riding and usually arranged to meet halfway between our homes, which were a distance of a mile for each of us - give or take a few hundred feet. We'd ride up the hill toward the old Womrath Plantation, or we'd head to another friend's house which was a couple of miles away on the old road to Aiken. Corn fields were plentiful along both routes.

1

Alice Twiggs Vantrease

One summer day we were riding toward home when a strange man in a raincoat jumped out of a corn field, yelling unintelligibly. He was naked under the raincoat, except for his brogan shoes and the hat on his head. He kept opening and closing the raincoat while he yelled at us. We couldn't understand what he was saying.

We calmed our spooked horses, and I said, "Let's act like we don't see him." My friend agreed, and we rode on toward home. We weren't shocked, just surprised an adult would act so silly.

Little did we know our decision to ignore the Corn Field Flasher would be the worst one we could make. It would only incite him to bigger exhibitions.

The next time he appeared we ignored him yet again. We did notice he quit wearing the hat. It was a plus that the horses weren't scared too badly either.

Regardless of which road we took that summer, he would jump out of a corn field when we passed by. It became so frequent that even the horses were no longer spooked. We wondered if he was leaping out at anyone else, but no one said anything about it, so we didn't either.

The man acted crazier and crazier with each flashing episode and eventually quit wearing the raincoat, although he did keep on the brogan shoes. One day he jumped out shaking a tambourine at us; on yet another he rang a cow bell and whistled "Dixie." One time he appeared playing a toy bugle off key; it hurt my ears, but I didn't look.

Nevertheless, we continued to ride horses, he continued to leap naked out of corn fields, and we continued to ignore him. It seemed like the right thing to do.

At the end of the summer the Corn Field Flasher appeared to us one last time. He jumped out, naked as usual, and ran around in circles yelling gibberish; this time he was shaking corn stalks in his hands while blowing a whistle – the kind you get on New Year's Eve or at birthday parties. He still wore the brogans, and we still acted as if he were invisible.

We never saw him again after that summer and suspect he found a more fertile field beside which to display his wares. We couldn't have driven him crazy because he was already there. He must have given up on us.

Our parents were unaware of his odd behavior since we never told them about it. We had a sixth sense that it would cause a problem: Our fathers would have been tempted to kill him, and Lord knows what mental trauma we would have endured when interrogated about the incidents.

The Corn Field Flasher hadn't traumatized us; we thought he was an idiot. We weren't old enough to be afraid of a naked man. We were country children and used to seeing all sorts of strange things.

Now that I think about it, he probably retired from the corn field and ran for public office. Politics is a profession where a person can get away with being an exhibitionist as well as a weirdo with naked ambition – figuratively speaking, of course. So - the next time you hear a politician speaking gibberish, consider the source and remember the Corn Field Flasher.

The Messin' Potion

I don't know what came over me that day. It was tax season, and I was nose-deep in financial records when Marie came into the kitchen. Marie was my housekeeper and a good friend as well. She was quieter than usual and stood at the sink pretending to wash a few dishes.

We went on this way for quite a while: I ignored her; she kept waiting for me to notice her – washing dishes, dusting countertops, opening and shutting the pantry door.

When her efforts to distract me failed, she said, "Where you been, Miss Alice?"

"To voodoo school," I answered. Like I said, I don't know what came over me. I had been out of town for over a week, and this was my first day home.

"You been where?" Marie wasn't sure she'd heard me right.

"To voodoo school. I've been to voodoo school." I figured that answer would shut her up. She was a firm believer in the voodoo power of "root" and knew not to mess with anyone who had access to that type of knowledge. The reference to "root" worked. She left the room.

It was quiet for almost an hour before Marie returned to the kitchen. Once again she began shuffling around the room arranging things. She worked in a slow frenzy for three or four minutes before she finally came up behind me and said, "You been to "root" school? You been there, sho 'nuff?"

I stopped working and turned around. She was staring at me differently from before – almost reverently. I hadn't counted on this consequence of my put-on; Marie believed I had the power of "root." There was no use to deny it now; she wouldn't believe me.

"Yes, Marie," I said, "I've been to voodoo school. Why?"

Her brows drew together, and she thought long and hard before saying, "Shorty ain't been messin' with me no mo'." Her face was glum.

I didn't respond to her comment too quickly. That would have insinuated I wasn't taking her claim seriously. In ordinary circumstances Marie wouldn't care one way or the other whether anyone was messing with her. She had been married numerous times. Shorty was her seventh husband. But she and Shorty were newlyweds: they had been together only about a month. I remember asking her one time how she could afford all the divorces she'd had. "Oh, no, ma'am," she'd answered, "I doesn't believe in divorce." She was very emphatic about that.

I pursed my lips to the side and knit my brows together before saying, "What do you think is the problem, Marie? I mean the problem between you and Shorty?" I was a newlywed myself, so I didn't have much experience with dysfunctional sex partners.

"I don't know, Miss Alice," Marie said, "he just ain't interested in me at all. He don't pay me the attention he used to." She had tears in her eyes. "Do you think somebody's already put the "root" on us? His ex-wife is mighty mean."

The mention of the ex-wife complicated the situation, so I knew I should be cautious: She had already made a voodoo connection with Shorty's behavior. I knew anything I did would have to work in sync with whatever potion had already been applied to her situation.

"Tell you what, Marie," I said as I got out of my chair. "I'll fix you up a potion. Take it home with you tonight and try it out. If it works, then it will mean the ex-wife hasn't put the "root" on you; if it doesn't, then we'll try something else."

I walked over to the cabinet above the kitchen stove and said, "Get me a half-pint jar and some spoons. Let's see what we can do."

Marie retrieved a canning jar from the dishwasher along with several spoons and handed them to me. She was grinning, yet apprehensive.

I pulled out about twenty cans of herbs and spices. I don't remember exactly what I used, but I do remember putting in oregano, paprika, thyme, pepper, and salt. When I had filled the pint jar to its brim, I put the cap on tightly and handed it to Marie.

"What do I do with it?" she said.

From the nether regions of my brain came the answer: "First, you can only use red meat. No chicken and no pork." I knew she wouldn't have any red meat in the house and she'd have to go buy it. A good meal never hurt any relationship. "Next," I added, "you have to season the meat with the potion and cook it just like he likes it. Add two potatoes and some green beans, and that should do the trick."

Marie's eyes were dancing. "Thank you, Miss Alice. Thank you," she said.

"You're welcome," I said and went back to my tax preparation. I didn't think about the potion again until the next day when Marie was late to work. She was never late to work.

When she walked in the door, she looked like someone had turned her upside down and shaken her. Her hair was unkempt, her clothes were wrinkled, and her eyes were bloodshot.

"Good Lord, Marie, what happened to you?"

Marie leaned against the kitchen wall and said, "Shorty, Miss Alice. It's all Shorty's fault. He ain't quit messin' with me all night."

I was shocked. "He what?"

"He ain't quit messin' with me all night. That potion sho do work. And if you think I looks bad, you oughts to see my landlady."

"Your landlady? What's she got to do with it?" I was confused.

"I had to give her half the potion to take me to the store to get the red meat." She reached in her pocketbook and took out a Kleenex. "When I left home this morning her husband was still chasin' her. I could hear 'em clean across the yard."

Marie looked so tired that I said, "Do you think you need to go home and rest today?"

She sat down in a chair, wiped the the beads of perspiration from her forehead, and said, "No, ma'am, I had to come to work to get some rest. That's a powerful potion you done mixed up."

"Well, there then," I said, "you don't have to worry about the ex-wife do you?"

"No, ma'am. She must not've put the "root" on us after all." Marie rested for a few minutes, then she went to work washing clothes.

I'm still wondering what in the hell I put in the jar. I've reached the age where I could use some of it myself.

The Hootchie Coochie Pickler

"You'll never win the County Fair pickling contest, Trixie. Miz Gunther's won it the last three years," Agnes said, "She's a good ol' girl. So ... why even try?"

Trixie wiped away tears said, "But I've got to. I've just got to win. Al thinks I can't do anything like his momma did." She looked back at Agnes and said, "I'm afraid he's going to divorce me if I don't win that pickle contest." She leaned down on the table and began sobbing loudly, causing two pigeons nesting on the window sill to fly off in fright, leaving two hungry squabs alone for the moment.

"Don't be silly, Trixie. Al would never divorce you. Why, you're the best thing that ever happened to him. The very best thing. He could've spent his whole life farming right here in Little Egypt, Georgia, and never found the happiness he has with you." Agnes leaned over and patted Trixie's heaving shoulders. "There ... there ... now quit your crying. All that sobbing won't solve a thing." She handed Trixie another Kleenex. "Now dry those tears. Let's make a plan. If you think you can win, well ..." Agnes paused and added, "You'll just win. That's all there is to it."

"Al's momma was the best pickler in the state," Trixie said. "My Al's proud of that."

"Yea, but she's deader than a doorknob now. Miz Gunther's the new pickling queen. She was talkin' about herself in the beauty shop yesterday. She had that little fyce dog of hers in her pocketbook."

Trixie sat up in the chair and wiped her face again. Her thick, black mascara had come loose, and her cheeks had a gray pallor from the constant wiping away of tears. Her bright red, curly hair was in disarray too. "I want Al to be proud of me," she said. "I've just got to win."

Agnes nodded and walked to the sink to get her friend a glass of water. She loved Trixie ... she really did, but sometimes Trixie was a dreamer - even irrational when it came to pleasing Al. *Guess her high-strung nerves come from being in show business*, she thought. Agnes had never seen Trixie dance at a Hootchie Cootchie Club, but she'd heard about it. She'd also heard Al complain about Trixie's cooking.

As she handed Trixie the glass of water, she said, "Trixie, do you even have a good pickling recipe?"

"Yes. 'Course I do. I copied one out of my grandma's cookbook before she died. I don't know what made me do it." She sniffled and said, "I just knew I would need it someday. I really did. My guardian angel must've been workin' overtime."

"Don't know 'bout a guardian angel, Trixie, but if you've got one, call on her now. Miz Gunther's won the pickling contest for the past three years ever since your Al's momma died. Three years in a row. Think of it ... three years in a row. Her pickles are the prettiest I've ever seen." She winced and glanced over at Trixie. "Not to say that yours won't be pretty too, mind you."

"Don't be apologizin' to me, Agnes. I know I've got hard work ahead of me, but I'm going to plant my own okra and make pickles from a home-grown crop."

"When you startin?," Agnes asked.

"Soon's the ground thaws. Al said he'd plow me up a little garden patch. He thinks he's humorin' me. All he ever says is 'whatever makes you happy, sugar.'" Trixie shook her head. "Imagine that. Him sayin' 'whatever makes me happy.'" She began sobbing again. "It'd make me happy if he liked anything about my cookin' ... anything at all. I'm just sick of hearin' about his momma and her good cookin' ... and I'm really sick of hearin' 'bout those damned okra pickles."

"I know you are. Have you picked up the entry blanks, rules, and regulations for the contest?" Agnes asked.

"Not yet. I called about them, but they won't be ready 'til next week."

"You've got plenty of time then. Tell you what ... I'll get 'em for you. I'm drivin' into town next week, and I'll go right by the fair grounds."

14

"Thanks, Agnes. You're really my best friend. My very best friend. I don't know what I'd do without you."

Agnes was not only Trixie's best friend – she was her only friend. Everybody in the beauty parlor said Agnes was the most open-minded woman in town, partly because of her friendship with Trixie and mostly because Agnes knew everybody's business. The townspeople looked on Trixie as a tarnished woman because of her past. It didn't matter at all that she'd snagged the richest bachelor in town; she was nothing but a honky-tonk woman to them.

Agnes sighed and looked at her watch. "Oh, Lord, Trixie. I've got to get to work." She picked up her bag and gave her friend a kiss on the cheek before heading to the door. "You just work on it, honey chile. I know you'll do the best you can. I'd like to stay here with you, but I've got an appointment to give a perm to that squirrelly little woman down at the Chevron station. Don't know why she gets 'em. She doesn't have much hair left. I've told her fryin' her hair won't help what's left, but she doesn't care."

Trixie called out as Agnes got in the car, "Her hair looks like a bird's nest when you've done with it."

"Yep. She tries hard to look good, though." Agnes said. "Even so, she sure couldn't work down at the Hootchie Cootchie Club. She'd starve to death."

Trixie laughed loudly at the thought of the Chevron woman dancing at the Hootchie Cootchie Club. Trixie didn't know much about pickling, but she knew a lot about dancing and entertaining men. That's how she met her husband. She had moved to Little Egypt from an even smaller town to further her career as a burlesque dancer.

Trixie knew she was in trouble the first time she saw Al. Big - Time - Trouble. She had put on twenty pounds, and her dance outfit – what there was of it – was too tight. One wrong move and it could explode off her body, leaving her naked and defenseless against the leering farmers and truckers waiting for her nightly performance at Big John's Hootchie Cootchie Club just off of the interstate near the first exit ramp to town. The town was twenty miles from where the County Fair took place every year – a venerated event to everyone in Little Egypt.

Trixie tugged on the side straps of her G-string; they held fast, and she finished dressing, putting on a skimpy see-through dance skirt and high-heeled black patent leather shoes. A jumbo-sized dance top to cover her huge breasts and an elaborate hat completed her outfit. Being totally naked in front of anyone was Trixie's biggest fear, even though she was now working far from home. She had promised her dying momma before she left home that absolute nudity was where she would draw the line in her profession as an exotic dancer.

The Baptist minister in the room also promised Trixie's mother he would see to it that Trixie stayed on a straight and narrow path. He kept his word. He started hanging out at the dance club until he finally lost his job after the church treasurer discovered the minister had put the entire proceeds of the church bank account in Trixie's garter: One hundred dollars a night until it all ran out.

It wasn't Trixie's fault, but church members blamed her just the same, and when a visiting trucker told her that a little club in Georgia could use a talent like hers, she headed for Little Egypt and a brighter future at the Hootchie Cootchie Club. She was the club's top performer in no time at all. Unlike other club dancers who appeared for work all tarted up and reeking of perfume, Trixie came to work looking like a school teacher dressed in a white, up-to-the-neck, long-sleeved, buttoned-up shirt, below-the-knee black skirt, sensible shoes, black horn-rimmed glasses, and had her hair in a bun at the nape of her neck. When she came out on stage, she was transformed into a Las Vegas-style showgirl. Her curly red hair was long and gorgeous and styled fully about her angelic face. She wore a headdress with pink ostrich feathers leaping out of a pink rhinestone hat. Her unblemished body had Rubenesque proportions, and her lavender eyes were bewitching behind long, false eyelashes. Her face was made up in a professional manner, and patrons of the club knew they were in the presence of an authentic exotic dancer. She was the biggest talent ever to appear in Little Egypt. The men at the club were wild about her.

Trixie had a rule against going out with patrons. "I don't believe in consortin' with customers," she said to anyone who asked. Yet she noticed a handsome farmer who began coming in every Wednesday night after she had been working at the club for only six weeks. She knew he was a farmer right away. "He just has that farmin' look," she told another dancer. He didn't say much, but every now and then he'd stick a twenty-dollar bill in her garter belt and say, "Thank you, ma'am. You've done some fine dancin' tonight."

Trixie learned his name was Al Lynwood. He was fifty years old and a confirmed bachelor. His mother had died recently, and he was living alone in the family home on his huge farm.

When Al started coming in on Saturday nights as well as Wednesdays, Trixie began to talk to him between performances, and they became friends. Nothing else happened. Al was too shy to put any romantic moves on her; she was afraid she'd lose her job if they started carrying on.

One Saturday night when Trixie was leaving the club after removing her makeup and putting on her school-teacher garb, she found Al waiting for her outside. "You look nice when you dress like that, Miss Trixie," he said.

"What?" She couldn't believe she heard what he said.

"You look nice tonight ... dressed up like you are now."

"What?"

"I said you look real pretty dressed like you are tonight."

"Thank you, Al. That's real sweet. I've just got on regular clothes ... nothing special." She reached up to her face and said, "I'm a mess. I don't even have on any makeup." She knew she was blushing.

"You look beautiful to me," he said. "Would you like to have a cup of coffee down at the diner?"

"Sure," Trixie said and they headed out into the night.

Three weeks later Al asked Trixie to marry him, and when she started crying and said "yes," he gave her a two-carat solitaire diamond ring he'd bought the day before at the only jewelry store in town, which is why all the townspeople knew what was going on before Trixie found out. The rumor mill was working overtime: Al was marrying a burlesque dancer.

Early in their marriage Al began giving Trixie hints about taking cooking classes. She tried very hard, but her food tasted awful and wasn't up to the food he'd eaten at his momma's table. When she asked Al to prepare her a garden one day just before the start of spring, he agreed. "Sure hope it makes her happy," he told a friend. "I don't know what's got her goat so bad. She's hell-bent and determined to pickle something. I wish I'd never told her anything about momma's okra pickles. I like pickles but not enough to cause Trixie any misery."

After Trixie planted the garden, the sunshine and rain ensured that the okra crop grew just as it should, and the okra developed into the perfect size for pickling. Trixie practiced pickling okra all summer and gave jars of it away to anyone who would take them. She didn't know what they did with them, but no one complained about them to her. Her friend Agnes finally refused to test the pickles because she said her mouth was going to turn inside out if she ate another one.

When she finally felt that she had perfected the pickling process, she made plans to pick the perfect, tiny okra pods for the next three days and then pickle them for entry in the fair. Nobody had told her that fair officials never tasted okra pickles; they just looked at the contents and color of the pickles in the jar. For all they knew, the okra could be pickled in almost anything.

Trixie got up the next morning and seemed so happy that Al gave her an extra kiss goodbye and patted her on the bottom twice before leaving for the tractor shed. Trixie put away the breakfast dishes, grabbed her gardening gloves and a basket, and headed to the garden. She couldn't believe what she saw when she got there: the okra was covered in a black soot-like substance, and the leaves of the plants were wilting. "Oh, my God," she said. "I've got to find Al. Oh, my God."

Al knew Trixie was distraught when she drove up to the shed. He got in the car and took her back to the garden plot.

"Too bad, sugar," he said. "You've just got a speck of bad luck. A blight's taken over your crop. We'll just have to try again next year."

Instead of crying, Trixie took on a determined look and delivered Al back to the field before going home to change clothes and head for Agnes's place to have her hair done.

"Dear God," Agnes said when she heard the news. "What are you going to do?" They were the only two in the beauty shop.

"I don't know. I just don't know."

"Lean back into the sink and let me put some extra shampoo on you."

"Ouch," Trixie said.

"Sorry. My hand slipped. Didn't pull out but a few hairs. Don't want you looking like the Chevron lady. Now what are you going to do about the okra?"

"Agnes, I said I don't know. I don't have any okra to pick. I've already called the grocery store, and they don't have any that's not old and bruised. What do you think I should do?"

Agnes put a towel around Trixie's head and said, "Go on in and sit in my chair while I look for the Little Egypt Shop-and-Sell. They might have an okra ad in there."

When Agnes came back she was grinning. "Look right here, Trixie," she said and shoved the paper in front of Trixie's nose. "Here's an ad for a new farmer's market right down the road. It's only fifteen miles away. They've got okra listed too. Besides that, you probably won't run into anybody you know and can still say you grew them yourself."

"Oh, no, Agnes. I could never do that."

"Too bad you can't find a jar of pickles that Al's mom fixed. Have you looked in your closets? We know you could win with her pickles." Agnes laughed out loud and dropped the shampoo bottle.

Forty minutes and a blow-dry later, Trixie was headed to the market. When she got there, it was closing. She yelled, "Wait. Wait. Do you have any okra?"

"Nope. Fresh out," the woman said.

"Oh, Lord. What am I going to do? I've got to find some good okra. Do you know where I might find some?"

"Try Barclay's U-Pick-It. It's four miles further down the road. They might have some."

Trixie returned to her car, and the woman finished closing up. A few minutes later Trixie spied Barclay's. It was still open.

"Do y'all have any okra to pick?" she said.

"Yes, ma'am. Sure do. Right over there to the left of the field. You need a bag?"

Trixie took a bag and headed to the okra stalks. There were only two pickling days left before the entries had to be in.

When she arrived home, Trixie was itching from her efforts at okra picking. She emptied the pods into a sink full of cold water and ran upstairs to take a bath.

After she fed Al supper, she added salt to the water and left the pickles in the brine mixture overnight. Al was already asleep when she got in bed, so she climbed in quietly and went to sleep. She forgot to set the clock.

It was noon the next day when she woke up. Trixie threw on her robe and ran downstairs to the waiting okra pods. She pulled out her pickling equipment and spent the afternoon producing six perfect jars of pickles. She was still in her night clothes when Al returned home.

"Jesus, Trixie. You been in bed all day?"

"Nope. Just finished pickling okra." Trixie held a jar out to him.

"Those look great, honey. Can I taste one?"

"Not until they set a spell. They're still warm. Give 'em time to cool."

"I'm proud of you, honey," Al said. "Real proud."

They spent the remainder of the evening playing dominoes. The next morning Trixie threw on jeans and headed to the Fairgrounds with all six jars. Wanting to be sure to enter the right jar in the fair pickling competition, she stopped at Agnes's house to get advice on which jar looked best.

"They all look good to me," Agnes said and covered her eyes. "Eeny-meeny-miney-moe ... pick a pickle jar by ... the ... top. This is the one," Agnes said and uncovered her eyes.

"Very funny," Trixie said and left with the pickles.

At the fairgrounds forty-five minutes later, Trixie had a hard time finding someone to point her to the area where the canning competition was to be held. Entries had to be in at noon, and she had five minutes left. She finally found one man leaning against a fence who pointed at a white building with a tin roof. "It's right there under your nose," he said.

Fair officials were closing the door as she walked up to the display shed. "Wait!" she called, but the door kept closing. She ran and stuck her foot in the door to keep it from closing. When it closed on her foot anyway she screamed, "Ouch! Ouch! Oh, my God. You've shut the door on my foot!"

The door opened quickly to the admiring glances of two fair officials she recognized from her days at the Hootchie Cootchie Club. "You hurt, Miz Lynwood?" one said.

"No. I'm just fine. I just need to get these entered in the pickling competition."

There were only two entries in the pickled okra section – Trixie's and Miz Gunther's. Trixie looked at both jars and was relieved that hers looked just as good as Miz Gunther's. But her jar was shinier too.

While the men commented on how fine her pickled okra looked, the women looked away and turned their noses up, whispering among themselves. Trixie didn't care. She headed for home and the judges went to judging. The winners would be announced that evening after the fair opened.

It didn't take but a few minutes for the women to vote on giving Miz Gunther the blue ribbon for the fourth year in a row. Agnes, who was on the committee, jumped in and said, "Now are y'all voting for Miz Gunther because she has the best pickles or because you want to spite Miz Lynwood?" She gave the women her most condemning stare, and they discussed the situation a few minutes before voting and giving Miz Gunther the blue ribbon again. It didn't take any special talent to recognize which pickles belonged to whom. A red ribbon was placed on the top of Trixie's pickles.

One of her male admirers walked over and looked at the pickles. "Why'd this one get the blue ribbon?" he asked.

"It's the best color, that's why," a judge said.

Trixie's admirer picked up the winning jar and for some reason turned it upside down and noticed a red streak on its bottom. "What's this red mark for?" he asked.

The other judges crowded around and looked at the jar. No one said anything. They just looked at each other in silence.

"I know what it's for," Agnes finally said.

"What?"

"It's the mark that means the jar has been entered into a previous contest."

"How can she do that?" the man asked.

Another voice boomed in. "She can't. It's against the rules." It was the pigeon-breasted president of the Little Egypt Pickling Club. She walked over and snatched the blue ribbon off Miz Gunther's jar and slapped it atop Trixie's.

"This other jar is disqualified," she said. "It doesn't get any ribbon."

"We can't just not give Miz Gunther a ribbon. This might be her last year of ever entering a pickle contest. She's old as dirt," said another judge and slapped the red ribbon on Miz Gunther's pickles.

Al heard the good news right away. One of his friends at the fair called him up and shared the pickling results. He came home early and found Trixie in an anxious mood.

He kissed her on the cheek and said, "Trixie, do you want to go down to the fair tonight? We can eat supper there and see how the pickling contest turned out."

"Okay, Al, but I told Agnes I'd run over to her place for a few minutes. I'll be back before long."

Agnes was waiting for her. She told Trixie all that had happened at the judging. "Miz Gunther was almost disqualified for re-entering pickles, but they gave her a red ribbon anyway 'cause she's so old," she said. "You're a blue ribbon winner, honey."

Trixie was silent. "No, I'm not. I'm not the winner," she finally said. "I won by default, and that's no win at all. If I can't win fair and square, I don't want to win at all."

"But you did win fair and square. You put all that work into your pickles."

"Well, Miz Gunther did too. She just did it another year. She's so old she probably picked up an old jar instead of a new one. I'm sure it was an honest mistake."

"Trixie, Miz Gunther wouldn't know an honest mistake if she tripped on one and broke her nose. I'm sure she knew exactly what she was doing."

"Maybe so," Trixie said. "I've got to head home, but I need to run by the store first. I'll see you at the Fair later. Al and I are going tonight."

Agnes arrived at the Fair a few minutes before Al and Trixie. She headed for the Home Economics displays where she met a group of the judges. She was at the door when Trixie sneaked up behind her and said, "Boo."

Agnes jumped and said, "Lord, woman, you just about scared me senseless." Al, as usual, said nothing, but he gave a broad grin and tipped his hat at the judges.

The judges were already there shaking their heads and murmuring among themselves. One motioned Agnes over.

"Where's your jar, honey?" Al said.

"Right there in front of you, Al. It's the one with the red ribbon,"

"Red ribbon?" Al was confused. "Red? I thought you got a blue ribbon."

"Sh-h-h-h-h-h…, Al. Don't say anything out loud. I did get a blue ribbon, but I sneaked in over here this afternoon and gave it back to Miz Gunther."

"Why'd you do that, Sugar?"

"If I can't win the blue ribbon because I really made the best pickles, I don't want it." She leaned over and whispered in his ear, "Besides, Miz Gunther was going to be real embarrassed if she lost, and I didn't want to be blamed for it. She broke the rules, and I didn't. People already talk about me behind my back, and she's so old I just don't think it would do her any good to be laughed at."

Al squeezed her hand and said, "Now see there, honey? That's why I married you. You're a good woman and a kind one, too. I don't know why you wanted to make those pickles anyway."

"Well, the sun don't always shine on the same dog's tail. My turn's coming up," Trixie said. Then she laughed and said, "C'mon, Al. Let's go eat some cotton candy and ride the Ferris wheel."

Before they left, she turned to the judges and said, "Evening, ladies. Do tell Miz Gunther I send her my congratulations for all her good efforts, and y'all too."

With amusement Agnes watched them walk away. Al had an extra spring in his step, and Trixie's walk was more voluptuous than usual. She laughed out loud when Al gave Trixie a little pat on the butt as they closed the door.

The judges were silent, either from surprise or embarrassment. Regardless, the high road had been staked out in Little Egypt, and Trixie had taken it. Agnes knew Trixie would win the next year, and the judges did, too.

The King of America

The telepathic message said *"Archeologists discovered The King of America today."* *The remains were exhumed from another time capsule found in the southern section of what historians believe to be a portion of the ancient United States of America. While the corpse had decomposed, a diamond-studded headdress remained intact and has been sent for immediate testing by the World Antiquities Lab.*

It's the year 4053, and news of the discovery is swift. The story is delivered through mega telepathy to all humans worldwide. Mega telepathy, information transmission from a central source to tiny computer chips implanted at birth in each human brain is proving a valuable aid in the worldwide effort to eradicate ignorance. There are no school drop-outs, and all humans have a Ph.D. by the time they are twenty-five.

Several weeks later, another mega telepathy message is transmitted: *Testing is complete on the headdress from what is now called the King of America Time Capsule. After thorough testing in the World Imaging Lab, scientists have determined that the shiny objects on the headdress, originally identified as common diamonds, are actually quartz crystals, well-known throughout the ages for their significance in historic events. Testing is ongoing on the DNA collected from the king's time capsule. Scientists are certain they will be able to accurately reveal the historical significance of the man in the magnificent headdress.*

In the year 1973 Jim Turner, an elderly farm laborer, was convinced that he could not see. All of his friends were wearing glasses, yet he was not. Fortunately he worked for Mr. Warren Jenkins, an optician who was sympathetic to his plight. Mr. Jenkins, upon witnessing the sudden onset of Jim's eyesight problem, immediately made an appointment with an ophthalmologist to give the old man an eye test.

On the morning of the appointment Jim put on his one gray, pin-striped suit, a white dress shirt, and a navy blue tie. The pants were too long and puddled around his ankles, obscuring his black-and-white saddle oxford shoes. The outfit was his Sunday best. On weekdays he wore an undershirt, overalls, and brown brogan shoes with the sides cut out to allow room for his corn-laden toes.

Jim arrived early for the appointment and decided to bide his time by visiting Mr. Jenkins, whose optical company was situated on the ground floor of the medical building.

"Good day, Mr. Warren," Jim said when he stumbled in the door. He was holding on to the walls and taking tiny steps forward.

"Good morning, Jim," Mr. Jenkins said, "Do you need some help getting to the elevator? I can have someone walk you over to it."

"Yes, sir. That would be just fine. My eyes seem to be worser when I'm inside."

The appointment was an hour away, so Mr. Jenkins began asking Jim questions about his eyesight. "When did you first notice the problem, Jim?"

"I first noticed it when I was hitching up the horse to the wagon. I couldn't see nothing. I missed the right hole to the harness cinch, and a big blister sprung up on Old Pet. I can't use her no more 'til it goes away. I been putting salve on her though. Don't you worry none about it."

"Do you have any other symptoms?"

"Yes, sir. I'm stumbling up and down steps. I have to have help in almost everything I do. I can't even see the sun when it comes up."

"Well," Mr. Jenkins said, "we'll have to have handrails put on the stairs to your house."

"Yes, sir, that would be fine. It sho' would help me."

They continued their conversation until time for the appointment. Jim was back downstairs within the hour.

"What'd he say, Jim?" Mr. Jenkins asked.

Jim staggered against the wall and said, "He said my eyes is perfect. Said nothing's wrong." Jim shook his head and tears welled in his eyes. "But there is something terrible wrong. I can't see nothing." He was squinting and had his nose against a picture. "I can't even tell what's in this case."

Mr. Jenkins called the doctor's office. When the receptionist answered, he said, "May I please speak to Skinny." Skinny was the nickname for Dr. Wellington, the portly ophthalmologist.

"Skinny," Mr. Jenkins said, "I'm here with Jim Turner, and he says you found nothing wrong with his eyesight."

When the conversation ended, Mr. Jenkins turned around and said, "Dr. Wellington says your eyes are perfect. He says you have the best vision he's ever seen in a person your age. Your vision is twenty-twenty on the chart."

"Well, they ain't. I can't see nothing." Jim's eyes were closed from squinting. He drew his brows together and pursed his lips in frustration.

Mr. Jenkins thought about it for a minute, and then said, "Tell you what, Jim. I'll make an appointment with Dr. Roulet."

"Okay," Jim said and walked around holding on to the wall, squinting, and stumbling until he reached a chair. He carefully held on to the chair's arms and moved his rear end slowly into position before plopping down. He was facing away from the sun, but he was still squinting. He picked up a magazine from a side table and held it up so close to his eyes that it touched his nose. "I can't see nothing," he said.

Dr. Roulet agreed to see Jim that same afternoon. Jim stayed seated in the chair waiting until time for the appointment. When Jim returned the results were the same: He had perfect vision.

Jim's response was the same too: "I can't see nothing." His bottom lip was quivering.

"Tell you what, Jim," Mr. Jenkins said. "Try on these glasses. See if they help you any."

Jim put on the glasses and his face lit up with a smile. "Yes, sir. I can see perfect now."

Mr. Jenkins pulled a case out from under the counter and placed it in front of Jim. "Look at these frames," he said. "Choose any frame that you like. I'll give them to you."

Jim looked over the case of frames and didn't find anything that pleased him. "None of these seem to suit me," he said.

As soon as Mr. Jenkins pulled out another case of frames, Jim turned around and spied a pair of glasses on a display mannequin in the far window. "Oh, Mr. Warren. I sees the ones I want. They are beautiful."

He was pointing to a pair of haute couture glasses made by Schiaparelli. The frames were made of quartz crystals as was the huge rooster-tail swirl of crystals set on multiple lines of prongs on silver wires; the wires swept upwards from the left side of the frame several inches over the top almost touching the other side. Several of the other crystal-laden wires twirled off in strange directions as if a tornado had just hit them.

Before Mr. Jenkins could make a comment, Jim had walked over to the frames and put them on. "Oh, Lordy," he said. "I can see even better now than I ever could before. These are the perfect glasses for me."

Mr. Jenkins gave the frames to Jim. They had been on display for a few years and were ready to be replaced anyway. "Okay, Jim. Let me have them for a moment so I can fit them to your face."

Jim handed the frames over and stood by anxiously until they were properly adjusted and back on his head. "How much I owe you, Mr. Warren," he said.

"Not a thing, Jim. It's my pleasure to give them to you."

Jim practically danced out the door saying, "Thank you so much, Mr. Warren. Thank you so much."

Mr. Jenkins went over to the window and watched Jim walk down the street. Several repairmen were working in a manhole, and Jim had to detour around them. Mr. Jenkins was surprised when none of the workers looked up or even acknowledged Jim as he walked by with the crystal rooster-tail glasses - even when he turned around and walked backwards so they could get a better look at him.

When Jim had passed by the men the second time, he turned around and leaned over the manhole and stared at them. The men started laughing, and Mr. Jenkins could tell words were exchanged.

Jim strode back to the office with an indignant look on his face. "Mr. Warren," he said. "You've fooled me. These frames don't have no magnifier in them." Jim poked his index finger through the hole in the frame and almost punched his eye. "See. They don't got no magnifier in 'em."

"You said could see better with them than any other pair, Jim." Mr. Jenkins said.

"I can, but they needs a magnifier in 'em. Those men told me my glasses weren't no good without glass in 'em."

Mr. Jenkins scratched his head and said, "Jim. Those men don't know what they're talking about. Those are high fashion glasses. They are the latest thing in eyewear. The reason they don't have glass in them is because they are air-conditioned."

"They are?"

"Yes. They are. Don't let anyone tease you about those glasses ever again. They're just jealous, that's all."

Jim thanked Mr. Jenkins again for the glasses. He wore them the rest of his life. When it was time to bury him, his will stated that he wanted to wear the glasses in his casket, so he could "see good in heaven."

The last mega telepathy message issued about the time capsule find said: *The remains of the King of*

America were interred in a climate-controlled glass coffin today in the World Museum of Regal Artifacts. A physical facsimile of the king has been created through analysis of the DNA found in the time capsule. Since none of the king's original clothing was salvageable, archeologists have dressed him in the typical fashion of the period in which he reigned. World residents are urged to visit the exhibit which will be on display for the remainder of the millennium.

People who visited the display saw a well-groomed, elderly man wearing the sparkling Schiaparelli frames. He was attired in bright green, bell-bottomed pants, a yellow shirt with multi-colored embroidered flowers on it, black high-heeled men's shoes, and a heavy gold chain around his neck. He was holding a set of peace beads in his right hand. The clothing items were described on a card next to the exhibit as "typical attire of the time in which the king lived."

Charlie Baker's Garden

A lone blue hyacinth was all that remained of Charlie Baker. It came up each year at the edge of the lawn behind the bath house and bloomed there rarely noticed for almost forty-three years.

Sammie Jenkins discovered the hyacinth in the spring of her sixth year. She thought it was a piece of trash at first, but when she went over to check, she smelled the delicious fragrance of the bloom, then knelt down and pressed her nose to it. She stayed there for almost the entire morning and repeated the ritual every day until the hyacinth's bloom faded and the bulb's leaves retreated for the summer.

"Where'd it go, Jacob?" she asked the hired man who was working nearby.

"Where'd what go?" he said.

"The pretty blue flower."

"The one growing close to where you is?"

"Yes. Right here. This one." She pointed to the bright blue flower spike at her feet.

Jacob walked over to where Sammie was standing before saying, "That's Charlie Baker's hyacinth. It's the last one left."

"Who's Charlie Baker?"

"You wouldn't know him. He's been gone a long time."

"Where'd he go?"

Jacob knew he would have to be honest with this child; she was old for her years. "Charlie Baker died over forty years ago. He's gone to heaven to live with God."

"What if he didn't want to go?" Sammie said. "What if he didn't believe in heaven?" Her parents were atheists and didn't believe in much of anything.

Jacob knew the family didn't go to church. The one time he'd asked about it, he'd been severely reprimanded. He said, "It doesn't matter if a person wants to go to heaven or not. It's not up to them. God makes the decision."

44

"But we don't believe in God," Sammie said.

"Don't matter," Jacob said. "What you believe in don't make no difference to the Lord. He gonna love you anyway. If you lives a good life, God's gonna take you to heaven whether you wants to go or not."

Sammie couldn't wait to tell her mother that God was going to take her to heaven if she was a good girl. Then maybe her mother wouldn't spank her for being naughty. She was sure her mother wouldn't want her hanging around with God. She thought better of it after a few minutes; she didn't want her mother yelling at Jacob again for talking about God.

Jacob walked back to his work. Sammie followed close behind and said, "Where's he buried?"

"Where's who buried?"

"Charlie Baker."

"Don't know. That was 'fore my time here. The Bakers didn't live here long. They left after Charlie died. He was the only chile they had." Jacob stopped and leaned on his hoe. "Come to think of it, I seem to remember somebody sayin' they went back to Chicago. That's right. It was Chicago. Way up

45

there where they kill all them hogs and where the gangsters is."

The next afternoon Jacob found Sammie sitting in her swing humming to herself. "She's a sad child," he'd told his wife one day. "Her folks leave her all on her lonesome. It's a wonder she ain't ruint."

He walked over and said, "What you thinkin' 'bout, Sammie?" he said.

"God."

"What about him?"

"I was just wondering if God made the flower live so long because Charlie Baker died, or because Charlie Baker planted it." Sammie looked over at Jacob and said, "How'd he die? Do you know?"

Jacob knew, but he didn't know if he should tell her the truth or not.

"How'd he die, Jacob?" Sammie was persistent.

"In a hunting accident," Jacob said. "I'll show you where it happened some day."

"Okay." She pushed her swing off with her feet and said, "I'm going to swing as high as I can now to see if my feet can touch the tree leaves."

"You do that," Jacob said and walked away.

Charlie Baker's name wasn't mentioned again until the hyacinth bloomed the next spring. "Look, Jacob," Sammie said. "Come quick! The blue flower's back! It's back."

Jacob heard the excitement in her voice and walked over to see the bloom. "It smells good, don't it?" he said.

"It's beautiful. It's just about the best smell I ever smelled," Sammie said. She was lying on her stomach with her nose against the bloom. "I'm going to smell just like this flower when I grow up."

Jacob chuckled. "You do that, Sammie." He knew about women and their perfume. He'd never met a woman yet who didn't love it or a man either, for that matter – as long as it was on a woman.

"Wonder how long it'll last this year," Sammie said.

"Probably 'bout the same as last year," said Jacob.

One day after the bloom began to fade, Sammie walked up to Jacob and said, "Show me where Charlie Baker died, okay?"

"Okay, but you have to tell your momma where you're goin'. Charlie Baker died up in an old pine tree down by the creek behind the pond."

When Sammie ran back out of the house, she brought a walking stick with her. "Momma said to slap the bushes with this, Jacob. Snakes might be crawling."

"That'll scare 'em away. We can throw some sand at 'em too," Jacob said, and they walked down the path toward the old road that led to the slow-running creek.

It was quiet when they got there. It hadn't rained in quite awhile, and when they reached the old bridge, it was covered in pine pollen and moss. No one had been there in a long time.

"Look, Jacob, I can see your footprints like you're walking in snow," Sammie said as they began to cross the creek.

"What do you know about snow, Sammie?"

"Nothing. I just think this is how it looks, that's all – 'cept it's white." She put her feet down carefully in the dust on the bridge and compared the size of her feet to Jacob's.

The rutted road disappeared just beyond the bridge. Layers of pine straw covered the road's path until it could no longer be seen. A tall pine tree stood to the side of the road as it ended. Jacob pointed to the message carved on the trunk: 'C. B. Was Here.'

"This was Charlie Baker's favorite tree, Sammie. He was killed in this tree."

"How'd it happen?" Sammie ran her fingers over the carving in the tree.

"He was hunting with a friend and climbed up in the tree to get a better view."

"What happened then?"

"Slow down, Sammie. I'm getting' to it." Jacob took his cap off and sat down on his haunches. He pointed up to the tree limbs above.

"See that fork up there?"

"Yeah."

"That's where Charlie was sitting when he was shot."

"Shot? Who shot him?"

"Slow down, Sammie. It was an accident. His friend shot him by accident." Jacob explained how Charlie Baker saw a deer in the distance and urged his friend to hurry and hand him the shotgun. The friend eagerly handed the gun up, but forgot to hand it up with the barrel pointed down. The friend slipped and his finger jammed against the trigger and the gun went off.

"One blast ... that's all it took. One blast and it was all over."

"Is that when Charlie Baker went to heaven?" Sammie said.

"Yes. That's when it happened. His soul floated right up to heaven to be with God."

"What'd his parents do? Were they mad about him going to heaven?"

"No. They was glad he wasn't alone. Even though Charlie was an only child – like you – they were glad he was in heaven with the Lord."

Sammie fingered the initials on the tree trunk one last time before they headed back home. They talked about how many dragonflies were hanging around. "Those dragonflies are snake doctors," Jacob said and reminded her to rattle the bushes with the cane as they walked home.

The next afternoon after school Sammie ran over to where Jacob was working. "Jacob, Momma says the hyacinth couldn't have hung around forty years - long enough for me to see it. She says you're just making up stories."

Jacob shook his head. Sometimes he wished Sammie's mother would keep her mouth shut. Her negative comments made it tough on everyone around.

"Sammie," he said, "I was told about Charlie Baker's flower garden when I first came to work here; I showed up just after the boy was killed and his folks sold the place. There were lots more hyacinths then. Everybody said they were growing in Charlie Baker's garden. They said he loved flowers. Said he always loved 'em from the time he was a baby. Far as I know, that's the last one living. And that's the truth as I know it." Jacob walked away.

Sammie reached down and picked the faded bloom; a few bright blue florets remained on the stalk. She walked over and handed it to Jacob. "Let's put this on Charlie Baker's tree," she said. "Let's put it where he went to heaven."

"I thought you didn't believe in heaven."

"I don't, but Charlie Baker did, and this is really his flower. I'll bet he hasn't seen a flower bloom in a long time."

51

Later, when they had returned from visiting the tree and leaving the bloom for Charlie, Sammie walked back over to the hyacinth plant. It looked strange to her without the bloom. She stared at it for a few minutes and then went in for supper. She didn't go back to see it again until after it had gone away for the summer.

It didn't come back the next spring. Sammie waited and waited for it, but it didn't appear. Jacob watched her go over to the spot every day and then finally said, "It probably just gave up, Sammie. It'd been there a long time. Maybe it was just waiting on you to find it."

"But where did it go, Jacob? Where did it go?"

"I don't know for certain where it went, but I believe it might be up in heaven with Charlie Baker." Jacob knelt down beside Sammie. She was patting the spot where the hyacinth once bloomed. "Why don't we get you some hyacinths and plant them here? You can get them in all different colors - white ones ... pink ones ... yellow ones ... and blue ones, just like the ones in Charlie Baker's garden."

"When I took the flower to him, that's what did it, isn't it? That's what killed it." Sammie looked

52

up and Jacob noticed how frightened she was. "Does this mean God's going to come get me too?" she asked.

Jacob realized that Sammie hadn't heard a word he had said. "No, child. 'Course not. Not until it's your time. It just means ..." Jacob stopped to think of another reason the plant was gone. When it came to him he said, "It just means that Charlie Baker's job was done."

"Charlie Baker's job?"

"Yep. It was his way of making sure nobody forgot him and nobody forgot his hyacinth garden."

"I'm not going to forget him. Are you?"

"No. But what are you going to think about every time you see a blue hyacinth from now on?"

"Charlie Baker. As long as I live I'll remember him every time I see a hyacinth."

"That's his message, Sammie: Always leave something good behind for people to remember you by - just like Charlie Baker did."

Many years later, when Sammie was an old woman and Jacob was long gone, visitors to the old home place marveled at the hyacinth garden in the spring. Sammie still lived there and tended it every day. She grew pink ones, yellow ones, red ones, and purple ones, but only one blue hyacinth was planted in the garden; it bloomed next to a small sign that said "Charlie Baker was here."

Every year Sammie always grew an extra blue hyacinth in a bulb jar and kept it by her chair on the porch. She hoped after she was gone someone would remember her as well as she remembered Charlie Baker when the sweet fragrance of the blue hyacinth filled the air and the pine trees bloomed.

The Fourth Day Celebration

He never learned to read, so A. B. Germany memorized every big word he heard hoping people would think he was educated when he spoke. Problem was he didn't know what the big words meant, so when he said, "The flamboyant pitcher pot fell over and busted itself senseless," everyone knew he had knocked something over.

A.B. began doing house work when he was seventy years old. He had retired from Crook Brothers Masonry Company where he mixed concrete all day for bricklayers. "With a name like Crook," he said, "there was no way around doing an honest day's expectation of splendiferous vocation."

Tall and thin, with angular cheek bones and long arms and legs, A.B. drove slowly but walked fast wherever he went. There wasn't a lazy bone in his body. He was chocolate-colored – not black and not brown – but a dark chocolate color with brown eyes, and he had an engaging smile which he rarely used except on special occasions when he relaxed for a minute or two. An only child of parents who were also only children, he had no relatives and only a few friends left living.

A.B. worked Mondays, Wednesdays, and Fridays for Mrs. Angelo and Tuesdays, Thursdays, and Saturdays for Mrs. Lehman. He rested on Sunday morning and attended church on Sunday afternoon at two o'clock.

Each day, whether working or not, he packed his belongings in the trunk of his light green Chevrolet Impala with Cabriolet top. "My neighborhood is hyper-ventilating," he said. "If I didn't pack up my stuff and anesthetize it in the trunk, it'd be stole before I reticulated back home."

His belongings consisted of two church suits, three white shirts, a radio, a black-and-white television set, one pair of dress shoes, two pairs of work boots, and several changes of work clothes. He kept his other personal effects – underwear, socks, sheets, and towels - in a laundry basket that he also placed in the trunk of his car every day when he left home; dirty clothes were kept in a used Army bag and pushed to the back. He had a frying pan, a tin cup, two baking pans, one plate, one glass, and a set of eating utensils that he kept on the floorboard of the back seat. He hid his shaving kit under the front seat.

When A.B. showed up for work, it was always quietly and slowly. "I don't believe in referencing a car too hard," he said to Mrs. Lehman the first day he went to work for her. He was proud of his car and polished it every Saturday afternoon so it would be shiny and clean when he drove it to church.

Things went smoothly for A.B. and the women in the beginning. He never missed a day of work and was glad to swap days whenever either of the women requested it. There was some complaining over where he would work on Thanksgiving and Christmas, but he solved it by offering the women a half day each on holidays. That rule applied to all holidays except one: A.B. Germany never worked on July Fourth. "That's the day Mr. Washington freed the slaves," he said. "That's my holiday and the one I calibrate on my own."

One day Mrs. Angelo tried telling A.B. the Emancipation Proclamation was not delivered on July Fourth. She was planning her own Independence Day celebration and needed his help. She told him that the proclamation that freed the slaves was delivered on September 22, 1862 and had become official on January 1, 1863. It made no difference. He was certain of his facts, and no amount of reasoning could change his mind. "No, ma'am," he said. "I've got my facts stored reluctantly in my head. I know when I needs to canonize my freedom day."

Mrs. Angelo was irritated but called a catering service and celebrated July Fourth without A.B.'s help. He was there early the next day, however, to help clean up the mess. "The rumination of the festivities can be tremulous," he told her. Mrs. Angelo rolled her eyes and reminded him to polish the silver service and water the potted plants before leaving for the day. She was also careful to point out the silk flowers and tell him they didn't need watering. This reminder was necessary because he had thrown out a beautiful arrangement recently when it began to smell and she discovered the vase full of foul water. She didn't scold him for this mishap; she knew he was always trying to please.

Several weeks later A.B. was asked to work for Mrs. Lehman for an entire week: She was having an out-patient operation and needed someone to stay with her during the day. "I'm glad your ostentation came out all right," he said to Mrs. Lehman on her first day home.

"Thanks, A.B." she said, "I'm glad it did too. Would you make me a cup of de-caffeinated instant coffee, please?"

"Where's it at?" he said.

"Look on the counter top next to the stove. You'll see a jar there. Two teaspoons in hot water will be plenty."

A.B. called out a few minutes later, "The jar's empty, Miz Lehman. You want me to go get you some more?"

"That would be fine, A.B." Mrs. Lehman reached for her bag and handed him ten dollars. "Tell them you want Sanka brand. De-caffeinated. Sanka. Can you remember that?" Mrs. Lehman knew better than to write anything down and embarrass him.

"Yes, ma'am. I can remember that," he said and left to run his errand.

A minute or so later, he reappeared at the door and called through the screen, "What kind of coffee did you say to get, Miz Lehman? I forgot the name of it."

"De-caffeinated coffee, A. B. Sanka. Just tell them you want Sanka."

"Okay," he said and was gone.

When A. B. returned he proudly handed Mrs. Lehman a jar of Sanka.

"Well," she said, "you did remember the right coffee, didn't you?"

"Yes, ma'am," A. B. said, "I told 'em I wanted some coffee what ain't got no cafeteria in it, and they knew just what I meant."

Mrs. Lehman thanked him profusely, and he went to the kitchen and prepared instant coffee. After washing the windows in the front of the house and vacuuming the floors, he left for the day after Mrs. Lehman assured him that her husband would be home shortly.

"Okay," A. B. said, "I'll just promulgate on home and I'll see you tomorrow."

Almost an hour later he was back. "Miz Lehman, I'll be late to work tomorrow. It's the first day of the month, and I gots to wait on my little check." He wanted to remind her of the date because he didn't want her to think he was shirking his duties. He was very conscientious about that.

When he first began work, he informed Mrs. Angelo and Mrs. Lehman that he would be late on every Social Security day because somebody might steal his check from his mailbox. He didn't have a checking account; he couldn't write anything but his name and preferred to be paid in cash because he couldn't tell if he was paid the right amount or not when he was handed a check. He eventually began bringing his Social Security check to one or other of the women each month; he asked them to cash the check and trusted them to give him the correct amount of money.

The seventh year he worked for the women, A.B. developed a cough that didn't go away. Mrs. Lehman noticed it first and called Mrs. Angelo to discuss it. They agreed that he must see a doctor and

Alice Twiggs Vantrease

made him an appointment with a physician who was a family friend. The diagnosis was immediate: A.B. had congestive heart failure. He was given medication and told to change his diet.

The women decided between them that they were destined to enforce his diet and planned meals accordingly. No longer did he get fried chicken or fried pork chops for lunch. No fat-laden snap beans or turnip greens. No potato salad and no macaroni casserole.

The only day the women hedged on his diet was on New Year's Day. They both fed him hog jowl, collard greens with fatback, rice and gravy, cornbread and butter with pecan pie for dessert. A.B. always took his plate into the back yard where he sat on a stone bench by himself and consumed his meal after saying grace. He never would eat in the kitchen even in bad weather.

The only day A.B. hedged on his diet was July Fourth when he picked up a 12-pack of fried chicken from the Chicken Shack where he also chose side dishes of potato salad and macaroni and cheese casserole. "I'm planning a splendid allotment of delineations to eat," he told them about his holiday menu.

Until the last year of A.B.'s life, the women never knew where he celebrated July Fourth. His heart failure had become critical, and he was admitted to the hospital in late June. He asked a favor of Mrs. Angelo. "Can you keep my car in your back yard 'til I'm up to circulating it again?" he said. "I'm afraid it'd be gone if I left it parked where I live. All my stuff's in the trunk too."

His health continued downhill. "I'm procrastinating for health reasons now that I've got a rectangular heart," he told them, and the doctor said there was no way he could leave the hospital grounds on the Fourth of July.

When A. B. heard the news he was devastated. "I've got to have my Fourth Day celebration. I've just got to. This may be the last time I can do it," he said to the women every time they came to see him. When they saw tears in his eyes, they knew they had to do something to help him.

Mrs. Angelo and Mrs. Lehman pleaded with the doctor to let A.B. leave the hospital with them on July Fourth. The doctor agreed as long as A.B. stayed in a wheel chair and was out no longer than three hours. A.B. was elated at the news. "Please bring me my suitcase out of my trunk," he said to Mrs. Angelo and handed her his car keys.

On the morning of July Fourth, the women packed a picnic lunch of fried chicken, potato salad, macaroni and cheese and cupcakes decorated with red, white and blue stripes. After they brought A.B.'s suitcase to him, they left the hospital room while he dressed. When he came out, he was dressed in a navy blue suit with a red-striped shirt and navy bow tie with white stars on it. He had a small United States flag stuck in his jacket pocket. "I'm ready to go now," he said and sat in the wheel chair.

When they reached the lobby, Mrs. Angelo went for the car, and Mrs. Lehman waited with A.B. It was mid-morning so there was not a lot of activity at the hospital.

A.B. stood up when he saw Mrs. Angelo's car and he began to walk toward the door. His breathing was labored and he stopped when he reached the door and leaned against it until he caught his breath.

"A.B.," Mrs. Lehman said, "If you'll wait, we can wheel you out in the wheel chair."

He shook his head and said, "No ma'am, it's the Fourth Day, and I'm going to walk proud on the Fourth Day." He stood back up and walked through the door.

Mrs. Lehman raced ahead and opened the door to the front seat. A.B. looked at her curiously and got in the car.

When Mrs. Lehman was seated in the back, Mrs. Angelo drove off and said, "Okay, where to, A.B.? Where are we going to celebrate the Fourth Day?" She glanced over at him and noticed how tired he looked. His eyes were sad, and his shoulders drooped.

"Head down toward the river," he said, "and turn right on that road that goes up by the factories."

"Do you mean Factor's Walk?" Mrs. Angelo said.

"I reckon so," A.B. said. He was leaning to the side with his head against the window.

"Where do we go after we turn on Factor's Walk, A.B.?" Mrs. Lehman said.

A.B. sighed and sat back up. He held on to the dash with his right hand and turned sideways so he could see both women. "You count six paved roads and three dirt ones on the left 'til you come to the Cotton Branch Baptist Church, and you turn down the road past that church."

Mrs. Lehman was blushing because she knew she had embarrassed him by asking for specific directions. "Oh," said Mrs. Angelo, "Are we going to picnic at the church?"

"No, ma'am," he said, "close to it, though." He turned back around and leaned against the window and in a few minutes seemed asleep.

When they turned beside the church, Mrs. Angelo slowed down and tapped A.B. gently on the arm. "We're here, A.B. Where do we go now?"

A.B. sat up and pointed slowly toward the field behind the church. "Drive back there to that hedge row. There's a farm road behind it. You turn left down that farm road. I'll tell you when to stop."

When they turned onto the farm road, plum tree branches and blackberry vines scraped the side of the car, and the holes in the ruts made the ride bumpy. "I'm sorry 'bout this road," A.B. said, "And if I wasn't sick, I'd rub the scratches off your car like I did mine. I'll matriculate them for you when I feel better." He paused to catch his breath and said,

"Drive on around the side of the field 'til you get to the middle. You'll see a road through the field to that platitude of trees over there in the middle."

When they reached the turn, they drove to the edge of the clump of trees and stopped the car. Many of the trees were in bad shape: Some from disease; others from the ravages of weather. A spiked, wrought-iron fence enclosed a small space in the middle of the trees. The gate to the enclosure hung on one hinge and was held in place by Johnson grass growing on either side of it. There was no vegetation inside the fence. It was clear of debris.

A.B. was awake, but still leaning against the window. "Can you drive a little closer," he said. "I don't think I can stroll that far today. I'd like to go in the gate."

Mrs. Angelo drove closer to the gate, then turned the car around and backed up. "This will make it easier for you to get in and out of the car, A.B.," she said.

A.B. nodded and put one leg out slowly when Mrs. Lehman opened the door for him. He rested for a minute and then put the other leg out and stood up.

"Here, let me help you, A.B.," Mrs. Angelo said.

"Wait a minute," Mrs. Lehman said, "I'll get the wheelchair. It won't be hard to push here, there's not much grass to go over."

"No, ma'am," he said. "I'd rather walk inside. You can procrastinate the chair for me to sit in, but I'd rather walk inside." He began slow, deliberate steps to the gate and through it until he reached a clump of stones on the right side near the fence. "I'd like to sit here, if you don't mind," he said.

Mrs. Lehman pushed the chair over and he sat down. "Are you hungry? Do you want to have your picnic now?" she said.

"In a minute, Miz Lehman. I sure appreciate you and Miz Angelo gettin' me here. I just want to regenerate for a minute." He leaned out of the chair and brushed some dust off of a stone with his long arm.

When he did, the women noticed that the stones were inscribed with initials and dates: G.G. 1864; A.M. 1876; W.B. 1852. They left A.B.'s side and began to walk around the enclosure noticing for the first time that the stones weren't remnants from the clearing of the land, but markers – grave markers – some dating back to 1750 before the War for Independence. After waiting a few minutes, they walked back over to A. B. and said, "Who are these people, A.B.? Are they your kin folks?"

"Yes," he said quietly. "What's left of them." He sat quietly for another minute, and then said, "It's where I want to be buried too. Here with my folks. They're all here. All of them."

"Are your parents here, A.B.," Mrs. Angelo said.

"Yes. They're here." He pointed to two stones closest to his feet. They were inscribed C.G. 1960 and A.B.G. 1961.

"That one's my momma," he said pointing to C.G. "The other one's my father. His name was A.B. Germany, too, like my granddaddy and his granddaddy. I'm the tenth one named that in my family." A.B. wiped a tear from his eye. "My daddy didn't live long after my momma died." He pointed to a bare spot several feet away. "That's where I'll be planted, I guess. It's one of the few places left perplexed in the cemetery."

"But, A.B.," Mrs. Angelo said, "There are other places here.   Here is one close to your parents. Wouldn't you rather be buried here with them?"

A.B. smiled and said, "Sure would, but I've got brothers and sisters buried here.   They didn't live long after they was born and they didn't get remembering stones. I'm the last one to go dead in here.   That's the place I'm supposed to be."   He pointed at the same spot he had indicated before.

"What about these other open places?" Mrs. Lehman said.

"There are folks there, too." He said. "They are the folks that didn't get a headstone. Back in slavery days, most slaves didn't have a perpendicular last name and no saturated money for a proper burying. My people have been buried here since before the Fourth Day became important."

Mrs. Lehman was beginning to tear up. Her voice was quavering when she said, "A.B., what do you want on your grave stone?"

"Yes," Mrs. Angelo said, "We'll make sure you get whatever you want."

"No need to," said A.B., "I've already made arrangements.   It's all written down in my Bible.

You'll find it in the trunk of my car after I'm gone. My last will and testicle's in the Bible along with some other papers. You'll need those too. I'm not sure what they say, but the lawyer man checked them over and said to strangulate them." He was breathing hard from the conversation so the women didn't say anything else and went to the car for the picnic basket.

When they had everything in hand, they walked back over to where A. B. sat and found him asleep. They quietly put out the picnic cloth and put food on the plates before waking A.B.

"Lunch is ready," Mrs. Lehman said to A.B. When he didn't stir, she said a bit louder, "Lunch is ready, A. B."

He heard her this time and took the plate of food she offered. "Thank you," he said. "It looks gangrenous."

They ate slowly so that A. B. wouldn't feel rushed and when they were through, handed him a red, white, and blue cupcake. He smiled and said, "Better not have but one bite of this cupcake. The doc says I've got to get more serendipity with my food."

The women laughed and put away the food and repacked the picnic basket. "Let us know when you're ready to leave, A.B." one said.

"I'd like to spend a few more minutes here by myself, if you don't mind," he said. "I'd like to put this flag on my daddy's grave. Would you put it there for me, Miz Angelo? I can't reach it."

Mrs. Angelo stuck the flag in the ground by the grave stone and she and Mrs. Lehman took the food back to the car. They waited there for a sign A. B. was ready to leave.

Thirty minutes later he was still sitting in the wheel chair looking around the graveyard. While they were in the car waiting, the women commented on how quiet it was away from traffic.

Suddenly a deer appeared out of nowhere and was startled at the sight of A.B. The deer jumped through the trees and disturbed a covey of quail that took off simultaneously and flew toward another hedge row at the far side of the field.

The women watched the birds fly away and when they turned around saw A. B. aiming his finger at them like he was hunting, and he was laughing to himself. He looked over at the women and said, "Okay, ladies, I'm ready to go now. It's time."

As they drove back around the field, A.B. said, "Did you notice how that covey of quail took off? All at one time? Quick like?"

"Why yes," Mrs. Angelo said. "I did notice that. Wasn't that amazing?"

"Yep. I've always wondered how they do that. Fluttering off and agitating all at the same time," A.B. said. "My daddy said they was a lot like my momma when she got mad. He said she fulminated off in all directions too ... just like a bonafide covey of quail."

"The Lord works in mysterious ways doesn't he, A.B.?" said Mrs. Lehman.

She looked at A.B., but he was asleep again with his head against the window. He stayed asleep all of the way back to the hospital and didn't wake up when they stopped the car at the entrance.

"I'll get an orderly," Mrs. Lehman said. "You stay here with A.B."

Mrs. Angelo nodded and waited.

Several minutes later an orderly arrived and helped A.B. out of the car and into the wheelchair.

When the orderly offered to wheel A.B. back to the room, the women accepted.

"You don't mind, do you A.B.?" Mrs. Angelo said.

"Yes. It's late and we need to get home. We'll be over tomorrow to see you. Okay?" Mrs. Lehman said.

As the orderly began to wheel him away, A.B. gave them a rare smile and said, "Thank you for celebrating the Fourth Day with me. I appreciates it. It was almost like I was perculatin' with family."

When he had disappeared inside the hospital, the women dissolved into tears and hugged each other, both stating, "I don't know what we're going to do without A.B. Who'll clean the silver? Who'll edge the lawn? Who'll polish the brass for our Colonial Dames meetings?"

When the women were back at home they spent the evening telling their spouses about A.B.'s Fourth of July Celebration, and how he was the last person left in a family that was now congregated in an old slave cemetery. "I don't get it," Mrs. Angelo said. "I can understand visiting the cemetery, but why would he celebrate the Fourth of July there?"

At Mrs. Lehman's house they discussed the possibility that A.B.'s ignorance compelled him to mistake the Fourth of July for Emancipation Day and wondered if he had ever celebrated the Fourth with a fifth of liquor.

The hospital called Mrs. Angelo early the next morning to inform her that A.B. had passed away in the night. She in turn called Mrs. Lehman and they decided to get A.B.'s Bible out of his car and determine his final wishes about his funeral.

The Bible was exactly where he said they would find it. The pages were well worn and the women noticed that it had been printed in 1867. "It must be a family Bible," Mrs. Lehman said.

At the back of the Bible there was an envelope with "Last Will and Testament of A.B. Germany" written on the front along with two other documents. The documents were not in envelopes, and both were brittle and yellowed with age.

They read the older documents first. One was a discharge from the Continental Army made out to Pvt. A.B. Germany in 1776. Another was a paper giving the slaves in the Germany family their freedom on July Fourth 1777 for service to their country during the War of Independence.

"Well, I'll be damned," said Mrs. Lehman.

"I'll be double-damned," said Mrs. Angelo.

They read his will last. In it he gave instructions that he was to be buried with a graveside service at the family cemetery in the field behind the Cotton Creek Baptist Church. He requested that all of his worldly goods be divided equally between Mrs. Angelo and Mrs. Lehman with the stipulation that as long as they lived they would put a flag on his grave every Fourth of July. He left all of his money, which was hidden in the false bottom of his suitcase, to the authorities in charge of taking care of the family cemetery.

A letter from the attorney was attached to the back of the will:

To whom it may concern:

A.B. Germany requested that a tombstone be erected above his grave site in the Germany family cemetery in the field behind the Cotton Creek Baptist Church. He was emphatic about his choice of words to be inscribed on his tombstone. I counseled him that other words might be more appropriate, but he was adamant that his exact words be used.

Arrangements for the tombstone have been made with the Magnolia Granite Company and the tombstone is to be placed on the grave one year after Mr. Germany's burial.

"Good heavens," said Mrs. Angelo. "What in the world would A.B. have wanted on his tombstone?"

"There is no telling," said Mrs. Lehman.

One year later the women drove out Factor's Walk late in the afternoon and turned on the first road past Cotton Creek Baptist Church then drove onto the farm road behind the hedge toward the graveyard in the center of the field.

They saw the huge tombstone before they reached the enclosure. It was made of pink marble and had a tall angel with wings outspread reading a book on its top.

After parking the car, they walked into the cemetery toward A.B.'s grave site. The rustle of the wind blowing through the leaves of the ancient trees was the only sound interrupting the quiet of the

Alice Twiggs Vantrease

afternoon. Slivers of late afternoon sunlight seemed to point the way.

They read the inscription when they reached the pink marble tombstone:

Here Ruminates
A.B. Germany
And All His Kinfolk
Freed On The Fourth Day
By General George Washington
May They Resuscitate
In Infernal Peace
And
God Bless America

The Hunting Party

It wasn't on my bucket list, but going hunting with a bunch of guys was an invitation I couldn't turn down as society editor of our local newspaper. The sports editor had left the job for another opportunity, and my boss wasted no time in filling his shoes. He called me into his office and said, "Sarah, there is no one else to cover the field dog trials. Do you think you can do it?"

I thought of all the reasons I shouldn't accept the offer – I didn't know anything about field trials, hadn't ridden a horse in years, didn't have any hunting clothes, and I'd have to get a babysitter for my children if the event went past school hours – but none of these things mattered. I said, "Yes."

"Good," said my boss and thrust a book at me. "Here is some information on quail hunting. You might find it useful, and close my door on your way out."

I left and closed the door before opening it again. "When are the field trials, boss?"

"Oh, I guess that is something you need to know," he said reaching for a brochure on a heap of other papers on top of his desk. "Take this. It has all dates and times in it and -"

"I know," I said. "Close the door on my way out."

"Right."

I closed the door and returned to my office to read the brochure and check my calendar. The field dog trial activities started on Friday, and today was Thursday. Moreover, it was January, and it was cold. It isn't always cold in the South, but you can count on January to bring some miserable weather.

The Georgia Field Dog Trials is an annual event in Waynesboro, a little town close to Augusta, Georgia. It has been held for over one hundred years. I had heard about it, but I was never inclined to participate in the sport.

My boss must have called the person in charge of the event because later in the afternoon just before I left work, the phone rang, and it was Edwin Mixon, chairman of the trials and owner of the nearby Cade Plantation where the field trials were held. Mr. Mixon lived in Connecticut but spent the winter on his plantation. He invited me to a cocktail party the next evening at his home to meet everyone in the group before the actual field trials began on Saturday morning. I accepted.

Before picking up the children from daycare, I stopped by the library and checked out several books on field trials and quail hunting. I spent the evening poring over them after the children were in bed. By the next morning I had just enough knowledge about quail hunting and bird dogs to make me more nervous than before about the assignment. But accept I had, and I knew there was no way out of it.

My boss gave me the afternoon off when I told him I didn't have anything to wear to the cocktail party. "You'll think of something," he said.

I did. I pulled my one black cocktail dress out of the closet and steamed the wrinkles out of it. I did have to go to the store and buy some sheer, black hose to wear. Black high heeled shoes and my pearl necklace would complete the outfit.

My parents came by and picked up the children for the weekend, and I was now free to be a female sports editor at large.

The cocktail party was from seven to nine. I wanted to arrive fashionably late, so I left home at seven. Everyone was already there when I walked in. I now knew participants in field dog trials were an on-time bunch of folks; I also discovered their idea of cocktail clothes was casual dress just one step above blue jeans. I was dreadfully overdressed, and I was the only female in the room. An attendant near the door took my coat, and I was free to roam a room full of people I did not know.

"Look who we have here," Mr. Mixon said and pointed to me. "Come on over here, honey. Let me introduce you." He pulled me toward him and escorted me around the room to each and every man there. "This little filly is the sports editor for the newspaper," Mr. Mixon told them. "She is going to be with us for the entire time. I want y'all to help her out if she needs any help." He snickered when he said this.

To their credit, the men were nice, shook my hand, and made sure I had plenty to drink. A half hour after I arrived, a young man came over and introduced himself. "Hi, I'm Hank Calderon. I'm covering the field trials, too. How many have you covered?"

"None," I said. "This is my first one. Nobody else was around to do it." I saw no reason to lie. According to his accent this guy was a New Yorker, and it wouldn't take him long to discover I didn't know the difference between a flush and a point.

After a few moments, I said, "Where do you work?"

"*Sports Illustrated.*"

"*Sports Illustrated*?" My mouth dropped open.

"Yes. That's where I hang my work hat."

"Wow. That's some job."

"Yes. I guess it is, if you have to have one." Hank laughed and said, "You want another drink?"

"Please," I said.

We spent the evening talking about little or nothing, and before I left, Hank said, "You let me know if you need any help."

"You can count on it," I said, noticing his broad grin beneath deep blue eyes and jet black hair. "What time are you getting to the trials tomorrow?"

"Probably about five-thirty in the morning."

"Are you kidding me? Five-thirty in the morning?" I could not hide my distress at having to wake up early.

Before Hank could answer, Mr. Mixon walked up and said, "My son, James, will pick you up in the morning, if you like."

"Oh, that will be fine," I said. "What time?"

"Between five and five-thirty."

I took a big sip from my drink and said, "Okay. Does he have my address? 501 Whitlaw Street?"

"He will have it as soon as I give it to him," Mr. Mixon said and walked away.

"So you get to ride with James Mixon…" Hank said.

"I guess so. Do you know him? Is he here tonight?"

Hank laughed and said, "No. He isn't here. He seldom comes down to the South. He is a loner. Doesn't mingle with many people, but he will come into a large fortune when his father passes away. Only child, too."

I pursed my lips and said, "Money can't buy happiness."

Hank laughed louder and said, "No, but it can buy one hell of a definition of happiness."

The evening ended with us shaking hands and agreeing to meet the next day and compare notes. I went home, set the alarm, and read myself to sleep studying field trials and bird dogs.

The alarm went off at 4:30 a.m. I took a quick shower, ran a comb through my hair, put on a minimum amount of makeup, and went to the closet. I pulled out my old riding britches and a black flannel shirt to wear. Coupled with a pair of wool socks, short boots, knitted hat, and a down jacket, I figured I'd be as warm as I could hope to be.

James Mixon knocked on the door a few seconds after I put on my lipstick. I grabbed my purse, gave myself one last check-up-from-the-neck-up in the mirror, and opened the door.

To put it bluntly, James Mixon was just about the handsomest young man I had ever seen. Gorgeous. Captivating. Charming. He could have passed for the moviestar Tom Selleck. Since I was dumbstruck, he made the first remark. "I hope I'm not too early, Miss ..."

"Sarah. The name's Sarah," I blurted out.

"Nice to meet you, Miss Sarah," he said in a stiff New England accent.

"Please just call me Sarah," I said. "Miss is for old biddies or young girls."

"Sure thing," he said and escorted me to his large pickup truck and opened the door for me. A liver-and-white bird dog was sitting in the front seat.

"Get in the back, Henry," James said to the dog as he opened the door for me. Henry didn't move but looked reproachfully at me as if I were kidnapping his master.

"Back. Get in the back, Henry. Back," James said more loudly and Henry slunk into the second seat in the pickup.

"Now you can have a seat, Sarah," James said and held the door until I was in. He then walked around the front of the truck and got into the driver's seat.

As soon as he shut the door, Henry began to howl. Not a quiet, sad howl, but a loud, angry howl.

"Hush, Henry," James said. Henry ignored him and howled even louder. "Henry is used to riding in the front seat. He gets upset when I put him in the back. Don't pay him any attention."

"I can't help paying him attention," I said. "People along the side of the street are paying attention, too. It's as if we were getting ready for a parade."

I wasn't exaggerating. Lights were coming on, and people were standing on their porches or looking out of a window to see what the commotion was about.

"Why don't you let me ride in the back, and Henry can ride in the front seat," I said. It was a reasonable solution.

"No, ma'am," James said. "That would look ridiculous. Do you want people to think I'm gay?"

"No, but are you?"

"Am I what?" James said.

"Gay."

"Gay? You're asking if I am gay?" James slammed on the brakes, pulled over to the side of the road, and stared at me with a lopsided grin.

"I was just kidding," I said. "I was just trying to lighten up the situation. That's all."

Henry was still howling. More lights were coming on, and several people were now in their yards staring at the truck.

"Damn," James said. "That's some kind of joke."

"What?"

"I said that is some kind of joke," he repeated.

"What?" I was acting as if I couldn't hear him because the dog was howling so loudly.

James shook his head and leaned his forehead on the steering wheel. "Jesus, you can't make this up."

"Tell you what," I said. "Put Henry up here in the front with me. He can sit on my lap. Perhaps that will quiet him down."

"Are you sure you won't mind?" Before I could answer, James got out of the truck and beckoned Henry to join him. Henry jumped out excitedly and peed.

A short minute later, Henry was ensconced on my lap, and we were headed to the field trials. He was no longer howling but was wagging his tail instead and hitting the side of the door rhythmically. He could have been a drummer.

"What kind of dog is Henry, other than the obvious bird dog?" I said.

"German Short-haired Pointer. Raised him from a pup," James said and then was silent for the rest of the trip.

A heavy mist covered the ground when we finally arrived at the Cade Plantation. Trucks were parked everywhere, interspersed with a few Cadillacs, Lincolns, and a lone Rolls-Royce. Several men were already on horseback. Instead of parking at the edge of the field with the other trucks, James drove to the back of the ante-bellum home and parked there. A handyman came out to greet us, opened the door for me and Henry, and took the keys from James. The handyman was dressed like one of the jockey statues you sometimes see in antique shops.

We headed into the house where James's father stood in the entrance hall talking with several characters who were obviously involved in the field trials, judging from the clothes they were wearing. The smell of freshly fried bacon hung in the air, and we headed down the hall toward the dining room with Henry following along with us.

"Good morning, little lady," Mr. Mixon said. "Did you get enough sleep, or is this too early for you to be up?" He chuckled at his remark and turned back to his guests before I could answer.

James steered me to the room on the right. The food on the sideboard was overwhelming: bacon, ham, sausage, scrambled eggs, quiche, cheese grits, fruits of every kind imaginable, sweet rolls, and biscuits with assorted jams and jellies. The dining table held plates and sterling silverware with a fresh floral arrangement at its center. The heart of pine flooring was covered with a well-worn Oriental rug, and needlepoint cushions graced the chairs. The crystal chandelier sparkled. The room oozed Southern aristocracy, although the occupants were what the locals called Damned Yankees.

"Help yourself," James said and handed me a plate. "I need to check on a few things, but I'll be back in time to take you to the field."

He turned and walked away before I could answer him. Henry was still walking by his side obediently. I took my plate, turned around, and bumped right into Hank from the night before.

"Some spread, huh," he said.

"Yes, it is, but not shockingly so," I said.

"What does that mean, not shockingly so?" Hank said.

"Nothing in particular. I just guess that people with enough money can create the illusion of anything they wish."

"In other words, money can buy their definition of happiness," Hank said with his eyes laughing at me.

I didn't respond but rolled my eyes upward and helped myself to breakfast items from the sideboard. When my plate was almost overflowing, I looked for a place to sit and eat. Every seat inside seemed taken, so I headed to the glassed-in sun porch where I found one next to an elderly gentleman. He was dressed in a white linen suit and held a brass-handled cane in his right hand while he read a newspaper.

"Is this seat taken?" I asked.

"No. Help yourself," the man said and went back to reading his paper.

A servant came by offering Bloody Marys, orange juice, or coffee, and I chose orange juice. She set the glass down on the table next to me and said, "Enjoy yourself. I'll be back around shortly if you want a refill."

I said, "Thank you," and focused on breakfast. I was hungry and finished my meal quickly. Just before I went back for seconds, the elderly man said, "You bring a dog?"

"No. Why?"

"Just wondering. 'Cause there's dog hair all over your clothes. Thought you might be a dog handler," he said and went back to reading his newspaper.

I looked down at my shirt. He was right. I was covered in Henry's hair. Note to self: Do not wear anything black to a field trial ever again.

I looked around and saw that the room was thinning out, so I wandered into the hall again to wait for James or someone else to point me in the right direction. I didn't have to wait long. James and Hank appeared at the same time. Henry sat down by James' feet and thumped the floor with his tail.

"Ready?" both men said in unison.

"I guess so." I suspected they had not met before, so I introduced them.

James and Hank shook hands and I said, "Where to now? I need to be on time for the…"

"First brace," Hank said.

"Right," I said.

James scratched his forehead and said, "Tell you what, since Hank is covering the field trials for his magazine, why don't you two ride together? Did you bring a horse, Hank?"

"No, but John Owens offered me one of his to use."

"No kidding," James said. "Then you're all set." He grinned broadly and looked at me. "I don't guess you have a horse, am I right?"

"You know you're right, James," I said.

"No problem. You can ride one of ours. Walk on over to the stables with us, Hank, and you can take Sarah with you to pick up your horse. It can't be far away because John Owens is the Bird Planter this morning."

I retrieved my jacket and put it on. As soon as we began walking to the stables, I pulled on my hat and gloves. It was going to be a cold day.

Alice Twiggs Vantrease

A roan mare was saddled and ready for me when we reached the barn. "You know how to ride?" James said.

"Of course," I said and acted insulted.

"Okay, then this one may be too tame for you. Should I saddle another one with a little more spirit?" He was grinning again.

"No need. I don't want to show off in front of all these people," I said and got on the horse.

Hank took the bridle and began to lead us away from the stable. "See you later," James said and walked in the opposite direction with Henry.

We hadn't gone thirty feet when I said, "What in the hell is a Bird Planter?"

It was Hank's turn to laugh. "You really don't know anything about bird hunting, do you? A Bird Planter carries quail in a bag made for that purpose and heads out on the course early in the morning before anyone else is around. These birds can be put out any time less than 30 days before the trials start."

"That sounds like cheating to me," I said.

"No. No it's not cheating. He salts the course with them, so the dogs will have something to point and flush."

"Oh. I get it. If there were no birds to find, there would be no use to have the field trials."

"Right. You're catching on, Sarah."

"Don't humor me, Hank."

"I won't. Stay here while I go over and retrieve my mount."

I waited and Hank appeared a minute or so later on a black walking horse. "Follow me," he said. We followed a narrow dirt road toward a pine stand, and when we crossed through it, we found ourselves in a field where scores of men on horseback and a gallery of observers and spectators were waiting for the first brace to begin.

Dogs of all kinds were also on exhibit: English Spaniels, Springer Spaniels, Vizslas, Labrador Retrievers, Pointers of every size and description, Irish Setters, and more. There was even one Weimaraner on the course, that, although a handsome dog, seemed out of place.

I watched in awe as the pairs of dogs competed. Point, flush, shoot, and retrieve. Point, flush, shoot, and retrieve.

"How do they tell who has the best dog?" I asked Hank.

"It is sort of subjective. The judges decide on which dog puts on the best show, and that dog wins. They like a dog that has a lot of style and one that seems to enjoy the hunt."

I rode with Hank all day and asked him a thousand questions, which he answered good-naturedly. We did stop for a picnic lunch, and when the day ended, Hank and I rode back to the barn, and I returned my horse to the groom.

Hank said, "How are you getting home?"

"I assume James will take me, wouldn't you?"

"Guess so. Let me know if you need a ride tomorrow. I am staying at the Lakeside Motel where just about everyone else is staying."

"Thanks, Hank," I said and walked toward the house as he rode away. I smelled like a horse.

James was sitting on the back porch with a drink in his hand. "How'd your day go?" he said.

"Fine."

"Your horse do okay for you?"

"Just fine, thank you. She is a nice mount."

"Well, come on in the house, and I'll fix you a drink before we head back into town. What would you like?"

"Vodka. Rocks," I said.

We went into the den, followed by Henry, and I took a seat in a burgundy leather chair next to a steady fire. It was warm and felt good. What didn't feel good were my legs. I was already sore from riding all day. Henry settled down on the rug in front of the fire, groaned, closed his eyes, and seemed to go immediately to sleep.

The entire den was paneled with mahogany and trimmed in wood beading. The ceiling was made of mahogany as well, and the deep crown molding, also mahogany, was beaded with dental molding below it. A large stained-glass window with what seemed to be a royal crest in the middle, was on the outside wall. The actual bar ran along almost the whole wall opposite the window. It was a big room, and beautiful.

"This is an unusual room, James," I said. "Was it always this way, or was it added?"

"It was added. It was originally in a revolutionary tavern not far from here. It was torn down years ago, and a farmer stored the mahogany parts. He sold them to my father when he bought

Cade Plantation. My father had it reconstructed as authentically as possible."

"He did a wonderful job," I said, "or someone did."

"Make that someone. My father can't hammer a nail without a helper."

"Well, that's how I am too. I can't construct anything either."

James was pouring vodka into a glass but stopped long enough to give me one of his mischievous grins. "You constructed some children, didn't you?"

"Yes." I blushed from my toes to my nose.

"Well, that's something to brag about." James brought me my drink and handed it to me atop a linen cocktail napkin embroidered with the letter M. He sat down opposite me in the matching chair by the fire, put his feet up on a leather ottoman, took a long sip of his drink, and leaned back in the chair. Henry raised his head and went back to sleep.

"Tell me something, Sarah. How did you end up in Waynesboro? You don't seem like a farm girl."

Now it was my turn to laugh. "Farm girl? Fat chance, although I did marry a man who pretended to be a farmer. We divorced, and I stayed here because I didn't want to disrupt the children any more than they had already been upset by the divorce."

"I see. Do you like it here?"

"It's okay. There are lots of good people who live here and have become my friends."

"What about your job? Do you enjoy working at the newspaper?"

"I do. Not so much as society editor because it gets pretty boring, but I do enjoy writing feature articles and the like."

"What about the sports angle?" He was staring at me intently.

"The sports angle is really a joke," I said. "As soon as my boss finds a man who can write, I'll be out of the job and glad to lose it. I'm not a big sports fan."

"Me, either, although I do enjoy watching football sometimes." James leaned forward and took another long swallow from his glass. "I need a refill. What about you?"

"No. Not me. One is enough. I think I have to be up early tomorrow morning too."

"Yes, you do. It's one of the perils of field dog trials. Do you want me to pick you up again?"

"I hate for you to drive all the way into town. I can probably catch a ride or, better yet, bum a ride from someone else."

"No. I'll come for you. I'll be up anyway, and Henry will enjoy the ride."

He fixed another drink, and when I had finished mine, we left. He drove me home with Henry sitting in my lap. Then he walked me to the door and said good night.

When I closed the door, the weariness in my legs hit me full force. They were trembling. I took two aspirins, climbed in a hot tub, and fell asleep promptly. When I awakened a short time later, the water was cool, and I was shivering as I toweled off.

I put on my nightgown, set the alarm, and climbed into bed. It was only eight o'clock at night.

James was right on time. Unfortunately, I overslept. It was too cold to leave him standing outside, so I threw on a robe, opened the door, and invited him inside while I hurried to put myself together.

The second the door closed, Henry started howling. This time it was a forlorn, wolf-like howl.

"Oh, my God, James," I said. "How long will he keep that up?"

"As long as he can't see me, I'm afraid," James said.

I ran into my room, put my clothes on, ran a comb through my hair, and made a quick stop in the bathroom to brush my teeth and wash my face and hands. Today I was wearing jeans and a khaki shirt. I was hoping to disguise the animal hair that would undoubtedly accentuate my outfit before the day was over.

Henry was still howling. He was howling louder than ever. I grabbed my coat and headed for the door. Henry quit howling as soon as he could see James, but the neighbors were already up. Lights were on, and I could picture them giving me obscene gestures. No one in my neighborhood was an early riser.

Henry got into my lap, settled happily down, and we headed for Cade Plantation. After breakfast, James walked me to the stable where the same mount awaited me.

"Here she is," James said. "Hope you have a nice day in the saddle."

"Me, too," I said and, as soon as I was in the saddle, remembered that I had not brought any pain killers with me for my aching thighs.

"Okay, then, head on out. I think Hank will catch up with you at some point." He turned and headed to the house, Henry at his heels.

Sure enough, before I had passed through the first pine stand, here came Hank. "Good morning again," he said and tipped his hat.

"Good morning, Hank. Did you get a good night's sleep?"

"Sure did, but only after I burned the midnight oil writing notes for my article. How about you? How did you sleep after a full day in the saddle?"

"Oh, my God, I just went home and crashed. I didn't write anything down. Guess I'm not such a good sports writer, huh!"

Hank laughed out loud. "Not to worry. I'm sure you'll get it together before press time."

I must have looked perplexed because he added, "Do you think you are going to be able to put together a good article from what you remember?"

"I hope so. Good thing it's a weekly newspaper because if it weren't, I'd be up the creek without a you-know-what." Overcome with a streak of gut level honesty, I added, "Hank, I don't have a clue about any of this. When it comes to sports, I am as dumb as a sponge. Truth is, I suspect my article won't have a hint of reality in it." I shrugged my shoulders then thrust them downward in an effort to look dejected.

"I'm sure you'll do just fine," Hank said.

"Well, one thing's for sure -- men in this town think women in general are stupid, so my article won't disappoint many people."

"You're kidding me, right?"

"No, I'm not kidding," I said, and damned if I didn't start to cry.

Hank pulled up alongside me and patted me on the shoulder. "There,there. Don't cry. It'll be okay."

This made me cry even more, and I pulled my horse over to the side of the road. "See? See what you've done?"

"What I've done?" Hank said. "What the hell have I done?"

"You just proved my point. Now I know even Damned Yankees think women are stupid."

"Jesus, Sarah. I meant nothing of the sort," Hank said. His voice was so loud, his horse reared up and snorted a couple of times.

After a long silence, Hank said, "Tell you what, Sarah. I'll give you my notes, and you can do with them what you will. Maybe that will help you write a better article."

This gesture of pity and kindness made me cry even more, but I took him up on it to my everlasting shame. I wiped my tears away, and we headed toward the field.

It began raining heavily after lunch, so the field trials were called off for the day. By the time I reached the stable, I was soaking wet and shivering. Someone said it might snow, and I knew that was wishful thinking because it never snowed in Waynesboro.

James and Henry took me home, and after another long, hot bath, I went to bed early with hurting thighs and a throbbing headache.

The next morning, I felt like hell, and it wasn't because of my aching thighs. My nose was running, and I had a fever. I didn't have James' phone number and waited for him to arrive only to tell him I was literally "under the weather." He offered his condolences and left quickly because I didn't invite him in. There was no need to set off the Henry alarm and awaken the entire neighborhood for a third time.

My parents still had the children and for a fleeting moment, I thought about running away from it all and becoming a nun, but I called them instead and arranged for them to continue their babysitting. I didn't want to begin a round robin of sickness with them.

I was still sniveling two days later when the field trials ended. I had one day to write an article to meet the deadline for the paper. My small notebook was no solace for me when I sat at the breakfast table and contemplated writing. However, the bed beckoned, and I crawled back in it, pulled the covers over my head, and slept.

The doorbell rang late in the afternoon, and there stood Hank with a parcel in his hand.

"Wow, you're not going to win any beauty contests in that outfit," he said. I was wearing an old bathrobe and Mickey Mouse slippers, both favorites.

"I'm not going to win the Pulitzer for sports writing, either," I said. "Please come in."

105

Hank came in and closed the door behind him. I pointed him to a chair. "Have a seat."

"Can't," Hank said. "I'm in a hurry to catch a plane." He thrust the package at me.

"What's this?" I took the package and furrowed my brow.

"It's a copy of my notes. Heard you've been under the weather, so I hope this will help you."

My eyes misted up. "Thank you, Hank. You're the nicest Damned Yankee I've ever met."

"How many have you met?"

"Just one," I lied.

"Figures," Hank said and grinned as he opened the door to leave. He paused and said, "See you next year?"

"Doubt it," I said. "I'm sure we'll have someone else as sports editor by then."

"Okay, then we'll have to do dinner while I'm in town," Hank said. He turned and walked out the door.

I never heard another word from James Mixon. I had had my first and last howling, good time with him.

I wrote my article, and it was well-received. The boss said, "Sarah, you've done such a good job, I want you to do it again next year."

"No, sir," I said. "I'm allergic to horses, and the doctor says I have to stay away from them." I headed for the door.

"Too bad," the boss said. "You're a good sports writer. I couldn't have done a better job myself." He turned back toward his desk and said, "And, Sarah ..."

"I know -- close the door behind me."

"Right."

I closed the door. Not only in the office but on sports writing as well. It felt good knowing I didn't know a damn thing about field trials but knew someone who did. I went back to my office, wrote Hank a thank you letter, and left to pick up my children.

I had learned a lesson: Money might not be able to buy happiness, but friendship and kindness could.

The Changing of the Guard

It was going to be an early winter, and Mr. Jones, a disabled World War II veteran who served as the neighborhood guard, was warning everyone within hearing distance to stock up on food and water in preparation for the upcoming blitzkrieg.

"What's a blitzkrieg?" John Coskery asked his mother when he heard Jones' warning on his way home from school. Mrs. Coskery was a widow, and John was her only child.

"Where'd you hear that word, John?" his mother asked.

"From Mr. Jones. I'm going to help him celebrate next week."

"Oh, yeah? What are y'all going to celebrate?"

"We're going to celebrate the shrinking of the *Bismarck*."

"You mean the sinking of the *Bismarck*, don't you, son?"

"I don't know. What' a Bismarck, Mom?"

Elizabeth Coskery smiled at her son. She knew that he had a soft spot in his heart for Mr. Jones. "The *Bismarck* was a German battleship, John. The British blew it up and sank it before it could do any harm."

"Yeah. That's what Mr. Jones said. He said the British blew those German assholes out of the water."

Mrs. Coskery looked at her son sternly. "John, don't use that kind of language. It's inappropriate."

"Mr. Jones says it all the time."

"He might say it, but it's wrong. Don't you use that word. Don't even repeat that word."

John didn't repeat the word again, but he did learn other things about Mr. Jones' war.

"The Krauts are at it again," he said a few days later at supper time.

"What do you mean the Krauts are at it again?" Mrs. Coskery asked.

"They're bombing England. Churchill says they're trying to crush British morals."

"Morale, John. They were trying to crush British morale. The word's morale."

"Okay. British morale. Whatever that means."

"And John," Mrs. Coskery said harshly, "you shouldn't use the word "Kraut." It's demeaning. It's a trash word. Don't use it again. Okay?"

"Okay." John's head hung low. She could tell she had hurt his feelings. He hadn't known the meaning of the word "Kraut" and was only repeating what he had heard.

She reached over and caressed his shoulder. "Crushing morale means pushing someone down ... lowering their self-esteem or self-confidence." She paused and said, "Do you know how you feel when someone at school calls you an ugly name?"

"Yes, ma'am." He thought about how badly he felt at the moment.

"Well, that's how a German person will feel if you call them a "Kraut.""

"Okay, I get it." John gave his mother a slight smile.

She smiled back and said, "Now back to the word 'morale.' Remember what the word 'morale' means, okay? The Germans were trying to make the

English give up hope; that's what Mr. Jones meant when he told you about crushing morale."

"Okay. I get it. Thanks, Mom," John said and then he was out the door and running down the street toward Mr. Jones, who was working the evening shift at the intersection.

"Are the Germans still trying to lower England's ...," John paused as he searched for the right word, "... morale?"

"Indeed they are," Mr. Jones said. "It's the Battle of the Bulge and a terrible time for the British. The Luftwaffe is all over them."

"Luftwaffe?"

"Never mind. I should have said Kraut Air Force. The Krauts are bombing the hell out of the Brits. But they won't give up easily. Those Brits are tough as nails."

John looked up at Mr. Jones and said, "You shouldn't say 'Kraut,' Mr. Jones. It's not nice."

"Not nice? Who are you kiddin'? Not nice?" Mr. Jones shook his head. "Who told you it wasn't nice to call those thievin', murdering Germans 'Krauts'?"

"My mom."

"Your mom?"

"My mom."

"Well, you better set her straight. Tell her to get into the real world. We're at war with those bastards, and she'd better not forget it." Mr. Jones squatted down and looked John in the eye. "You tell her that for me. Okay? You tell her that those Krauts might be over here next week, and she better thank God that I'm on the lookout for them."

John said "okay", but he knew he wouldn't say anything more to his mother about Krauts. Nor would he tell Mr. Jones anything else his mother said, either. The adults were definitely on different wavelengths. He made a promise to himself that he would ask Mr. Jones when he didn't understand what things meant instead of asking his mother.

He was beginning to agree with Mr. Jones when Jones said, "You can't understand a woman. Don't ever try. They're friendly one minute and mad as hell the next."

John's assessment of women was further magnified when he came home a few weeks earlier with a badly skinned knee. His mother had become hysterical. "What happened, John? What

113

happened?" she kept asking. It was times like this that John felt uncomfortable and wished his father was still alive. He knew he was the "man of the house," yet he felt helpless.

When his mother calmed down enough to listen, John said, "Mr. Jones said to 'duck.' He thought he heard a bomb dropping. He covered me so I wouldn't get a direct hit."

By this time she was crying and hugged him closely. She wondered if Mr. Jones was becoming more unhinged.

The days became shorter and colder, but Mr. Jones stayed at his post regardless of the weather. He had a heavy wool coat that he wore unless it warmed up in the afternoon; he took it off then and wore a dark olive sweater until he was chilly again. When it was raining, he wore galoshes and a yellow hooded raincoat over his wool clothing. He and John continued their conversations every afternoon when John came home from school. When school let out for the Thanksgiving holidays, John spent several days guarding the intersection with Mr. Jones.

"I'm a buck private now, Mom," he said at Thanksgiving dinner.

"You are?"

"Yep. He enlisted me and four other boys. Mr. Jones says that smart men like us are just what the Army needs these days." He didn't add the rest of Mr. Jones comment: 'The Army needs plenty of buck privates to help kick Kraut asses.'

Mrs. Coskery knew her son enjoyed visiting with Mr. Jones, but she continued to worry about Mr. Jones' mental condition and wondered whether his behavior was causing John's imagination to work overtime. Just last month she had to repaint a neighbor's fence when John and his friends wrote "Kilroy was here" on it after being sent on a secret mission. She was also concerned that the boys and Mr. Jones were using passwords and developing a code to ensure that they could continue to communicate an emergency war situation.

Other neighbors were also concerned. Not about John or the other boys, but about the expansion of the veterans' home where Mr. Jones lived along with seven other mentally disabled war veterans. The owner of the home was petitioning the city for a license to increase the size of the house to allow the addition of up to ten more men. A neighborhood meeting was called for the first Friday evening in December ahead of the City Council meeting to be held the following Tuesday evening. All residents within a four-block radius of the home were invited to participate in the meeting.

On the day of the neighborhood meeting, John stopped by to discuss the war with Mr. Jones. A car had backfired earlier in the day, and Mr. Jones was shaking more than usual. "Are you cold, Mr. Jones?" John asked.

"No. I'm just nervous. The enemy likes to make sneak attacks. But don't you worry. I'm on watch, and nothing is going to happen to you. We've got the B-24 Liberators flying; they'll take out anything that gets near here."

"Thanks, Mr. Jones," John said. He didn't hang around and wait for the other neighborhood boys to help with guard duties. He asked for "time off" and walked home to complete his homework so that he could go to a cub scout Christmas party that evening. His mother was going to be out too, but he didn't know why.

Everyone in the neighborhood showed up for the meeting, including the newest family who had bought the house a block down the street from the Veterans' Home. "We don't want any more crazy people living in our neighborhood," the newcomers said to anyone within hearing distance.

By the end of the meeting, a resolution had been passed to urge the City Council to deny the request to enlarge the Veterans' Home. Several hot-headed people suggested asking the Council to condemn the property and get rid of the veterans altogether, but calmer people in the group were able to dissuade them. In Mr. Jones' lingo, the neighborhood was becoming a war zone.

When John came in for supper the next evening he announced, "Adolf Hitler killed himself today. He and that Evil Braun have gone to their reward."

"Did Mr. Jones tell you that?" his mother asked.

"Yep. Hitler was a chicken. He was afraid of the Russians. Can I have another biscuit?"

Mrs. Coskery did not pursue the subject further. John didn't either.

On Monday morning, John left for school as usual. When he got there he noticed the new

117

Mennonite girl in school crying. She had been crying every morning since she joined their class. He didn't like girls all that much, but walked over to her and said, "What's wrong?"

The little girl couldn't answer because she was crying too hard. Her hair was in pigtails, and she had on an old-fashioned, longer dress than the ones the other girls wore in his school.

"Quit talking to that weirdo, John," someone yelled. "Can't you see she's a religious weirdo?"

John turned around to see who was yelling at him. It was the neighborhood bully. "Get over here and quit talking to that nut," the bully said again. "Send her to school with her own people; she doesn't belong here with us."

The little girl kept crying, and John put his books down, walked over to the bully and said, "Stop it. She isn't hurting anybody. Keep your nose in your own business."

"You shut up," the bully said. "Look at what she's wearing. She doesn't belong with us."

"Stop it," John said again.

The bully reached over and shoved John backward. John regained his balance, came forward and slugged the bully in the face as hard as he could. Instead of fighting back, the bully backed up holding his hand over his nose, which was now bleeding profusely through his fingers.

A teacher heard the commotion and came running to them. She grabbed both boys by the arm and herded them into the school. John went to the principal's office; the bully went to the infirmary.

No one asked or cared why the fight happened. Both boys were suspended from school, and their mothers were called to pick them up immediately.

While John was waiting, his favorite teacher walked into the lobby outside the principal's office and asked, "What are you doing here, John?" It was unusual for John to get into trouble at school.

John told her everything. He told her about the new girl and how the bully had called her a religious nut. He told her about Hitler and how the Jews were treated. He told her about concentration camps and religious intolerance. He told her how he and Mr. Jones were committed to preventing anything like that from ever happening again. "It's

119

un-American," John said. "I'm not Neville Chamberlain. I don't believe in appeasement."

"I don't believe in it, either," the teacher said, "but sometimes it's best to walk away instead of getting into a fight."

"No, it's not." John said through gritted teeth. "Some people don't understand anything but strength. It's the first time I ever hit anybody. I had to."

The teacher continued to listen, and by the time Mrs. Coskery picked up her son, the teacher knew that Mr. Jones was an invaluable asset to the community and that his lessons to the neighborhood children were rare and priceless – although locked in history and somewhat skewed in time. His opinion of Germans was definitely out-of-date, but his moral lessons were timeless. She was aware of other school incidents where Mr. Jones' name had been brought up.

After school was out for the day, the teacher went back to the principal's office and shared John's story with him. The principal shared the story with the publisher of the *Waynesboro Journal* the next day at

the weekly Kiwanis Club meeting. It was Tuesday --
the day of the City Council meeting.

That afternoon the publisher of the newspaper
called his city editor and shared the story with him.
"Go investigate this Jones fellow," he said. "He's
having a huge influence on the children on Whitlaw
Street. I think he's living in that veterans' home
everybody is up in the air about."

The editor passed the assignment along to one
of his reporters, who spent all afternoon talking to
Mr. Jones and tracking down John and his mother as
well as other neighborhood children who had access
to Mr. Jones' war wisdom.

That night the City Council meeting was
heated. When no common ground could be found
among the parties about the veterans' home
expansion, the mayor tabled the subject until the next
meeting.

The next morning, Mr. Jones' picture was on
the front page of the *Waynesboro Journal* above the
fold. The article underneath the picture said:

"Is This Man Dangerous?"

*The people on Whitlaw Street think Roger Jones is a
dangerous man. He lives in the Veteran's Home in the 500*

121

block of Whitlaw Street and has a few people in the neighborhood out of sorts.

Jones is a veteran of WWII and received the bronze star, two purple hearts, and the oak leaf cluster. He is a hero by anyone's definition, yet he doesn't know it. He has shell shock. His heart and soul are trapped in a time warp caused by his mental anguish over the horrors of the war he witnessed. A war that took the lives of thousands upon thousands of soldiers throughout America. A war that caused sensitive men like Jones to prefer the solitude of living in the past to the anguish of living in the present.

Jones' brother died in the war; Jones came home a hero - along with other veterans to whom we owe much. But his medals from fifty years ago aren't the reason he's a hero today. He's a hero today because of the life he leads and the example he sets for the children on Whitlaw Street. Not in spite of his mental condition but because of it.

You've seen him many times. You've seen him standing at attention on the corner of Whitlaw and Fifth streets, saluting cars as they drive by and halting traffic so a child can safely cross ... perhaps your child.

You've heard him call out warnings when a storm is coming, you've heard him whistle loudly when a child is running too fast toward the intersection, and you've heard him cry when the pain in his memory overcomes him.

Yes. Jones is a hero today.

Why?

Just ask Elizabeth Coskery. She'll tell you why.

Ask her son, John Coskery. He can tell you why too.

They will tell you that Jones is a patriot who has never been a hypocrite or harbinger of ill will to another human being. He loves freedom and he loves fairness. He believes in telling the truth and confronting your enemies when they are wrong. These are the values he's taught the children on Whitlaw Street. It's a lesson learned well by young John Coskery, who took Jones' words to heart and stopped a classmate from being harassed because she was a Mennonite and dressed differently. It's a lesson learned by another child on the same street who urged his classmates to befriend instead of berate the first black child to integrate the classroom. It's a lesson learned by still another child on Whitlaw street who saved his money to buy new toys as Christmas presents for disadvantaged children and for yet another who writes letters for a blind child who also lives on Whitlaw Street.

Alice Twiggs Vantrease

These children are sending a message to the adults in our community and anyone else who believes Jones and others like him are a threat. Their message says that prejudice and bigotry is not okay; their lesson says those who served honorably in our country have the right to live honorably in our community.

Many of these veterans are now living the remainder of their lives out in our midst; they should not be shunned but embraced.

And when next you sing "God Bless America," think of Roger Jones and the gift he gives the children in our community. He's teaching them the lessons that many of us have forgotten.

The next time you pass the intersection of Whitlaw and Fifth streets, look for Roger Jones in his heavy wool jacket or yellow rain slicker. Tell him "thank you" and don't forget to salute.

Is this man dangerous?

The children on Whitlaw Street don't think so. We should listen to them. Sometimes children are wiser than adults.

Mrs. Coskery read the article over her first cup of coffee. She showed it to John when he came to the table.

By noon, every adult in Waynesboro was aware of Mr. Jones' lessons. At the next City Council meeting the veterans' home expansion was approved unanimously, and a resolution was passed to give Mr. Jones a key to the city.

By the end of the holidays everyone in the neighborhood had settled back down, and John was back on patrol with Mr. Jones. On New Year's Day John announced, "I've decided to go to military school. Mr. Jones says I'm never going to get anywhere as a non com. He says I'm a leader of men and that we've got to keep making the world a safer place."

Mrs. Coskery smiled and said, "You're right, John. We can't ever let others forget the lessons of our past." She silently thanked Mr. Jones for being a surrogate father to her boy. And she no longer worried about his influence on John's imagination.

1964 – A Memoir

When I first heard the screaming, I thought it was a screech owl then realized it was daytime and the owl would be asleep. I walked over to a window in the dining room and saw Marie running toward the house and realized it was Marie screaming.

"Miss Alice ... Miss Alice ... help ... Miss Alice ... help," Marie was running and yelling at the same time.

I ran out onto the front porch, but Marie had already turned the corner, headed to the back door. I ran back in the house where Marie and I almost ran into each other in the back hall.

"Miss Alice ...," Marie was out of breath. "Wilhelmina havin' her baby. She need help, Miss Alice."

"Slow down. Slow down and tell me what's wrong,"

"Wilhelmina's deliverin' her baby. We can't find the midwife. She need help. We gots to do something."

I was listening carefully to Marie, but it was hard to understand her because she was talking so fast. "Slow down, Marie, slow down and catch your breath," I said. She gasped for breath a couple of times, and when she was breathing half-way normally again, she finished her story: Wilhelmina's baby was being born, and Wilhelmina needed help. The midwife had been called but was not at home. She would be notified as soon as possible, but in the meantime, somebody needed to take care of Wilhelmina.

As newly-wed housewife, I didn't know what to do. In the rural Georgia countryside I had no close neighbors, and my friends were an hour's drive away.

Marie was still one step short of a full-blown fit, so I knew I had to remain calm. "Okay, Marie, go back over to Wilhelmina's house and stay with her until help arrives. I'm going to call Uncle Doc and ask him what to do. I'll be there as soon as I can. Tell Wilhelmina help is on the way."

When Marie left, I immediately called my uncle, a physician in Augusta. Luck was with me. He came to the phone right away. "Uncle Doc, Wilhelmina, one of the colored folks on our place has had a baby and ..."

"Slow down, Alice," he said, "Has the baby been born?"

"Yes. That's what I'm trying to tell you. Wilhelmina's having the baby and nobody can find the midwife." I was beginning to panic.

"Calm down. You say there's nobody there who can help with the delivery?"

"No, sir. Nobody."

"Okay, then you should to go over there and boil some water. Make sure everything is as sterilized as you can make it under the circumstances. Tie a knot in the umbilical cord close to the baby's navel and tie another one further up. Then call the hospital in Waynesboro and tell them about the situation."

129

"What kind of knot? I don't know what you mean?"

"It doesn't matter what kind of knot. Just tie a knot as best you can in two places. Do you understand? Two places."

"Okay. I'll do my best, Uncle Doc."

"That's my girl. Now go on over there and do like I've told you. Then put the mother and the baby in the back seat of your car and head for the hospital as soon as you can. Call me later and let me know how things are going."

"Okay, I will. Thank you, Uncle Doc." *Oh, my God,* I thought. *How am I going to do this? I hate the sight of blood.*

A couple of large towels were on top of the dryer, so I grabbed them and headed out the door leaving my handbag behind. I jumped into my car, backed out of the garage and headed to Wilhelmina's shack.

When I got there, an old black Ford was parked outside, and Marie was standing on the porch.

"What's going on, Marie?" I said.

"The mid-wife ... she just showed up. She's inside with Wilhelmina and the baby."

130

"Thank goodness," I said and then remembered that Wilhelmina's husband, Willie, wasn't there. "Where's Willie? Has anybody gone to tell him the baby's come?"

"He's still in the field. He won't be home 'til second dark. They're working over on the Dye place today," Marie said.

"That's right. I forgot." I remembered that my husband had said earlier in the day the crew was going to be plowing over on the Dye place. I knew it was useless to search for Willie; he would lose his pay for the time he was away from the field, and there was nothing Willie could do to help with the birth.

A few minutes later, a very small, elderly black woman in a black dress, black shoes and stockings and carrying a black physician's bag stepped out of the house. A white collar with lace framed her shriveled face.

"I've taken care of the baby. I think he'll be fine."

"He's a boy?"

"Yes, ma'am. He's a boy. Fine little fellow, too."

My relief must have been obvious, because the mid-wife chuckled and said, "Everything's just fine. No worrying need to be done now."

I exhaled and sat down on the front steps. "Thank God." I said a little prayer for Wilhelmina and the baby and thanked God again for good fortune in that the mid-wife had beaten me to the shack.

Marie came over, sat down next to me on the steps, and whispered, "Somebody's got to pay the midwife, Miss Alice. Willie ain't home yet, and payday ain't 'til Friday. I'd loan 'em the money, but I don't have any myself."

"Oh." I was startled. It hadn't occurred to me the mid-wife would want to be paid. "Well, okay. I'll pay her." I stood up and asked how much was owed.

"Twenty dollars for the birthing and five dollars for the silver nitrate for his eyes," the mid-wife said.

"You'll have to wait here until I go back to the house and get my pocketbook." I felt my face flush, and I didn't know why I was embarrassed. "I was in such a hurry I didn't bring it with me. I'll be right back with your money."

"Yes, ma'am. That'll be fine. I'll wait here 'til you get back."

I got back into the car and headed back to the house. I raced inside, found my pocketbook, and checked to make sure was enough cash to pay the woman.

After the mid-wife left, Marie and I went inside the shack to check on Wilhelmina. She was lying on a mattress with blue and white ticking stained with large splotches of blood and amniotic fluid. The baby lay in her arms next to her. Swarms of flies were buzzing around, and the smell was awful.

I felt the nausea rise up in my throat. "Excuse me," I said and ran outside and emptied my stomach. When I had finished retching, I went back inside and found that Marie had taken the towels and wiped off the mattress. It looked better, but the smell was still nauseating.

"Wilhelmina," I said, "are you going to nurse the baby?"

"No, ma'am. I need to get back in the field as soon as I can. I'm gonna bottle feed him."

"Okay." I looked around the barren room for baby bottles. Not seeing any, I asked, "Where are the baby bottles?"

"I don't have any."

"Well, where are the baby's clothes and diapers?"

"I don't got none of them, either."

Marie was standing by quietly with a sad look on her face. "She don't have anything, Miss Alice. She don't have nothing for the baby or herself. Is there anything you can do to help?"

I could tell it hurt Marie's pride to ask for help. "Of course I can help. You stay here with Wilhelmina, and I'll run over to Waynesboro and pick up some things for the baby. I'll be back before you can shake a finger."

It took about thirty minutes to drive to the Rexall drugstore on Liberty Street. I purchased a dozen baby bottles, extra nipples, a case of baby formula, and a bottle sterilizer. I noticed a sale on fly swatters as I was checking out, so I bought two of those. Next I walked down to Mack's department store and picked out three baby outfits and four dozen diapers. There was a small selection of diaper pins; I chose the tiny blue ducks because they were cute and because they were the only ones that looked right for a boy baby. There was a sale on sheets so I purchased a double bed set and asked the clerk to point me toward the rubber bed liners, which I knew would be needed. On impulse I also picked out a pretty pink nightgown and robe for Wilhelmina.

When I arrived back at Wilhelmina's shack, it was six o'clock. I had been gone just over an hour and forty-five minutes. Marie was still there and helped me unload the car.

I unpacked the fly swatters as soon as we were inside. Wilhelmina and the baby were asleep, so I whispered, "Marie, if Wilhelmina's not going to nurse the baby, we need to sterilize some bottles for her."

Marie looked at me like I was crazy. She didn't say anything, she just stared.

"What? What are you thinking? Tell me, Marie."

Marie pointed around the room. "There ain't no electricity, Miss Alice, and no running water, either. How're we going to fix up baby bottles with no electricity and no running water?"

135

I looked around the room carefully. There was no electricity. There was no running water. In fact, there was also no stove, no refrigerator, and no kitchen to put them in. *Oh, my God*, I thought. *Why didn't I notice it before?* The events of the day overcame me and I burst out in tears. "Oh, my God, Marie. I didn't realize. I didn't think ... I had no ..."

"Sh-h-h-h-h," Marie said, "Don't cry. 'Course you didn't know better. You hadn't been over here before, had you?"

I couldn't speak and shook my head "no."

"Well then, there's no need for you to be all crying. We can fix up the bottles in your kitchen, if that's all right with you."

I was still sobbing and nodded agreement. I was overwhelmed with the day's events. "That'll be fine, Marie. Let's just take them back over to the house. Maybe I can find a cooler for her to use." I looked around and saw that Wilhelmina was still sleeping. Several flies had settled on the baby's face, so I picked up a diaper and handed it to Marie. "I think you'd better put a diaper on the baby. Put another one over its face so the flies won't bite him." I reached into a bag and pulled out the set of sheets.

"If Wilhelmina wakes up, you can make up her bed, too. I bought these for her when I was in town. I bought some rubber matting to put under them, too."

Marie took the diaper and sheets and said, "I turned the mattress over while you were gone. Didn't want her lying in her mess any longer than she had to." Marie picked up the baby carefully. He squealed and peed in her face before she could cover him with a diaper. She laughed and said, "That's just like a boy, Miss Alice. You got to cover that thing up or he'll pee right in your face. You need to remember that when you get your own boy child."

I smiled and thought, *Jesus, after today I'm not sure I want a baby – boy or girl.* I picked up the dirty towels Marie had used earlier and put them in one of the now empty shopping bags. "I'm going to take these back to the house and put them in the washing machine. Okay?" I didn't know why I was asking Marie permission to wash, except that the laundry room seemed to be her special domain.

"You do that, Miss Alice, and I'll get Wilhelmina situated. I'll walk back up to the house in a little while."

After I parked the car in the garage, I sat in it for a long time before I went in and started washing the towels. I wasn't really thinking of anything. I was numb.

Several weeks later I saw Wilhelmina working in the cotton field. The baby was lying naked on a blanket in the shade under a nearby tree. I walked over to check on him. He was a fat little thing and seemed to be perfectly happy. A coke bottle full of milk with a baby bottle nipple jammed over the opening was lying beside him.

Wilhelmina, husband, and baby moved away a few months later. I went back to the cabin and found what few things they had left behind: the stained mattress, the sheets I had provided, and a few empty cans of food.

A year later someone said Willie had left Wilhelmina, and she had moved to Chicago with the baby. I never saw them again, yet it seemed as if they were always lurking around in my mind to remind me of how tough life was for farm laborers in those days.

From that point forward I knew babies could flourish in the worst circumstances. The birthing event also prepared me for motherhood when the time came ... I made sure I arrived at the hospital before my baby came into the world.

White Trash

It took twenty minutes to walk to the grocery store. Annie parked the baby carriage outside of the front door, herded her children together on the sidewalk, and said, "Y'all watch Little Willis. Stay right here 'til I get back." She checked her pocket and counted the coins: two quarters ... three dimes ... five nickels ... six pennies. She added them up in her head; she had one dollar and eleven cents, and the children were hungry. They hadn't eaten since breakfast, when they had only a half biscuit each with a dollop of jam along with a glass of water. Payday wasn't until Friday – two days away – and she had to make what little money she had last as long as she could.

Annie was a young woman, but she had poor posture, and her natural blonde hair needed washing, making her look at least twenty years older than her actual age of twenty-nine. She might have been attractive if she gained twenty pounds and put on a little makeup or had clothes that fit instead of wearing hand-me-downs that hung on her body like funeral drapes. The dark circles under her long-lashed hazel eyes were indicative of the life she led: working long hours in the daytime and getting little sleep at night.

She didn't have access to a car as her husband took their truck to work with him, so whenever they needed any groceries or other staples, she had to walk to town – five miles further down the road – or stop by Ogden's, which was a twenty-minute walk. She was grateful for the baby carriage and used it as a grocery cart when Amy stayed home with the babies.

Ogden's Grocery was about as far back in the country as a store could get. It was housed in a building that was constructed in 1890, flanked on one side by a vacant building that had once been home to the town bank. A drug store had once occupied the building on the other side; it was now used for storage.   A one-room post office and Turner's Mercantile Store sat across the railroad tracks.   In addition to selling dry goods, Turner's served as the loan company and wine and beer supplier to the community. There was no liquor store. The closest one was several miles away on the main road to Augusta.

Annie was disappointed there wasn't a liquor store in the crossroads town. Not that she ever drank whiskey; she didn't. The lack of a liquor store just meant the local moonshiners could charge more for theirs, and that meant her husband Willis brought home even less of a paycheck at the end of a week. "You can't keep a man from drinking," she told her children, "he can only stop himself if he has a mind to." Old timers said moonshine liquor made a man mean if he drank too much – that was certainly true of her husband. Moonshine liquor could also kill a man if it wasn't stilled right.

The acrid odor of DEF hung in the air. DEF was the chemical that farmers used to defoliate cotton prior to picking it.

Annie looked around the store as she went in. Not much had changed since her last visit. Huge wheels of rat cheese sat atop the counter; they were covered with cheesecloth to keep away the swarming flies. One side of the store was full of canned goods; the other contained baskets of onions and potatoes along the front wall, and further toward the back household products and personal health items could be found. There were several tables in the middle of the store; each contained an assortment of local vegetables and fruits. The meat counter was at the very back of the store, and the rank smell of freshly plucked chickens permeated the air. "I hope they sell those chickens today," Annie thought, "or someone's gonna be sick." The meat bins were cooled by blocks of ice. The electric motors had burned out long ago. The one electrical unit that was still working held the milk, cream, and butter.

Annie walked over to the canned goods section and noticed a sale sign under the canned salmon: two for eighty-nine cents. She chose one and then noticed a box on the floor that said "Damaged Goods." She searched through them and found a can of salmon with half the label torn off. She picked it up and put it in her basket and then carefully placed the other can of salmon back on the shelf.

The clerk behind the counter wore a baseball cap, jeans, and a white undershirt. Annie couldn't see his feet. She could tell he had a mouth full of chewing tobacco from the lump in his cheek.

"Hey, you," the boy said, "what you looking for?" Annie's throat dried up. She was easily intimidated and said almost in a whisper, "I'm just looking for a few things for our supper."

He glared at her and yelled, "Well, don't be putting your hands all over everything. Some people don't like felt-up food. And don't steal anything, or I'll call the cops."

Annie said, "Yes, sir. I'll get my things and get on out. I'm paying for what I'm getting." She knew rednecks liked to be called "sir." Made them feel important. She glanced down at her hands and noticed the specks of dirt under her nails. *Seems like I can't ever get them clean*, she thought, and curled her fingers into her palms to hide her nails.

A car pulled up to the gas pump in front and distracted the young man, so Annie went back to searching for bargains. Not finding any, she picked up an onion and four potatoes and carried them to the counter. She waited while the boy rang up the gas

145

sale and then placed the items in front of him. "I'll take these, please."

The counter boy weighed and priced the onion and potatoes and added the sale can of salmon. "That'll be a dollar and fourteen cents," he said.

Annie put her dollar and eleven cents up on the counter. "Guess I'll have to put back one of the potatoes," she said.

The boy glared at her and snatched one of her potatoes off the counter. He weighed and priced the potatoes again and said, "That'll be one dollar and eleven cents."

"But surely that other potato was worth more than three cents," Annie said.

"Take it or leave it. I don't care which." He threw the items in a brown paper bag and shoved them across the counter at her.

She took it and walked outside to her waiting children.

"I'm hungry, Momma," little Harry said. He was the oldest boy. There were two other boys - twins, but they were still toddlers – three years old - and they grabbed their mother's skirt as soon as she returned. Little Harry was seven. He was a handsome boy, but Annie couldn't get close to him. He had been an irritable infant and couldn't be satisfied. "He's too serious," her friends told her. Now that he was getting older, he seemed to take more and more pleasure out of taunting her and bossing her around. She knew he needed discipline, but she was too tired to apply it, and his father didn't think he needed it. *He's just a boy. Leave him alone*, her husband, Big Willis, insisted.

"I'm hungry too, Momma," Amy said. She was the only girl. She was thirteen years old and had been born when her mother was sixteen and before her mother met Big Willis. She was a quiet girl and a good one. She helped her mother without complaining and spent her free time looking through any magazines she could find.

The baby, another boy, was fast asleep in the carriage. His gaunt look was a result of too little food; the rattle in his chest and labored breathing was due to asthma complicated by exposure to too much dust in the cotton field. Annie put the grocery bag in the carriage and wiped the spittle from the baby's mouth. He wrinkled his nose and made a face but didn't wake up.

Alice Twiggs Vantrease

Annie herded her brood together and said, "Let's go home. I know you're hungry, and your daddy will be home soon. I need to get supper on." She gently took Amy's hand and placed it on the carriage handle. "Amy, you push the carriage, honey, okay? And Harry, take one of the twins by the hand. Make sure he doesn't get in the road. Somebody might be driving too fast. Might not see us. I'll hold on to the other one."

"Why do I always have to hold their hands, Momma? Can't Amy do it?" Harry was cranky from too little sleep and too much hunger. The twins, sensing his distress, began crying and tugged harder at Annie's skirt, wanting to be picked up and held.

"See, Ma? See? They don't want anybody holding their hands but you," Harry said. He kicked up some red dirt with his feet and took on a sullen look.

Amy stood by silently waiting for the argument to be over so they could head home. She knew she would have to peel the potatoes and slice the onions. Her mother hadn't told her what they were having for supper, but she didn't have to be told: salmon stew was a staple in their diet – when

148

they could afford the salmon. Otherwise, they ate boiled potatoes or drank the broth after it was watered down enough to go around.

Annie soothed the twins and took them by the hand. Harry was looking on in disgust. "Never mind, Harry. I'll do it. You go on ahead."

Harry didn't answer and took off skipping down the road. He was glad to rid himself of the situation. He wanted to get back home to the new kittens that were living under the back steps. *I've got to hide them before Pa finds them*, he thought. *Pa hates cats*.

"Be careful of cars," Annie called out after him. He didn't answer. His behavior aggravated Annie because she knew he had heard her. She was concerned his attitude toward her was getting worse, and she hoped he wasn't going to end up like his father – sullen and bitter about his lot in life and prone to drinking too much.

About halfway down the highway toward home, one of the carriage wheels fell off. The baby, jolted awake, began to cough and cry pathetically in a quiet mewing way. The twins joined in and, looking up at their bewildered mother, fell down onto the side of the road having a "full conniption fit" as country folks liked to call that type of behavior.

Amy steadied the carriage and tried to put the wheel back on, but the shaft had broken and the carriage was disabled, perhaps forever. "I'm sorry, Ma," she said. "I didn't mean to break it."

"You didn't break it, honey, it's just old. Old and tired like me. Come on – pick up the baby. I'll take the twins. Can you carry the groceries, too? We'll leave the buggy here and come back for it in the morning. Maybe nobody will steal it and your daddy can get it fixed." Annie blinked a tear from her eye and thought, *God, I hope we can get it fixed. I don't want to haul stuff around with an old grocery cart like some kind of homeless person.*

Amy picked up the baby and the bag of groceries. Annie held the twins tightly by the hand, and they walked along the dusty side of the highway until they reached the turn to their house.

The dirt road leading to the house was made of sand mixed with red Georgia clay. When the wind blew or when a car passed, it rose and covered everything like a fine red powder one might find in a clown's theatrical makeup kit. When it rained, the sand eroded and washed to the side, and then the clay took over and made the road so slick only cars with very good tires dared to travel it. It was cotton-picking season, so everybody wanted the rain to hold off. If it rained, none of the pickers could work and the cotton might mildew in the field. Annie secretly wished it would rain anyway. She was tired. Besides, if it rained, the children could play Indian and streak their faces with red clay war paint. She hadn't heard them laugh in a long time.

They walked a quarter mile down the dirt road to their house. It wasn't much to look at – a tenant house – a shack some people would call it – that had only rudimentary amenities. There was a kitchen, dining room, living room, and two bedrooms. The floors were made of heart pine and had been painted a rusty red. The knot holes in the floor had been covered with Band-Aids, and they were painted over with the same rusty red paint.

The house did have a bathroom, but none of the plumbing worked. There was an outhouse in the back – a two-holer – and any fresh water they used had to come from a water barrel at the corner of the house or from the pump which always needed priming. There was a windmill in the back yard, but it no longer kept the pump running and the water tank filled. Its blades just whirled around and around when the wind was blowing and creaked to and fro when the wind was low. An old hoot owl lived in the water tank where it made its nest. Annie was grateful for the owl; it kept the rats down in the yard. There was an old shed in the yard, too, but its roof had fallen in.

When they reached the house, Harry was playing with the kittens in the back yard. "Don't tell Daddy about the kittens, Momma, okay?"

"Okay, Harry, but you know we can't afford to feed them. You need to find them a home or your Daddy's going to find them sooner or later and he's going to kill them."

Harry picked up the kittens and started crying. "It isn't fair, Momma. It isn't fair. They ain't hurt nobody. They didn't ask to be born, and I didn't either."

Annie realized Harry was more upset than usual. "Just keep them hid, Harry. We'll figure out something."

Harry nodded and walked toward the shed cuddling the kittens in his arms. "I'll give you some of my supper," he said to them. He tucked them carefully into a box in the corner where he had placed fresh straw earlier to keep them warm.

In the meantime, Annie and Amy had settled in with the children and started supper. They didn't discuss it; they knew who was going to do what and when to do it. Change was not an option in their life.

Big Willis was getting off work at the same time his wife Annie was struggling with the kids and headed home with the groceries.

"Hey, Mr. Willis, you want me to gas up the tractor tonight or do you want me to wait 'til morning?" Willie, one of the black farm workers, said. Willie wanted to head home himself; his wife was expecting a baby.

"Suit yourself ... don't matter to me. I'm plumb wore out," Willis said as he walked toward his baby blue Ford pickup truck parked under the shade of the live oak behind the tractor shed. A bird had crapped on his windshield, so he drove his truck over to the water pump and washed it off before heading down the road toward home. It wasn't a new truck, but it was a reliable one. It didn't give any problems, and Willis could count on it to start in any kind of weather.

He turned on the radio and tuned in to a country station. A commercial was on, so he punched up a couple of other stations until he gave up and turned the radio off. It was dusk, and he had about a thirty-minute drive home. He glanced down at the seat beside him and picked up the *Playboy* magazine he had found in the trash at work the day before. He turned to the centerfold and salivated. He had to swallow to keep the spit from running out of the corners of his mouth.

Willis was horny. He felt his crotch and the hardening bulge growing in his pants and adjusted his testicles. "Jesus," he said. "I've got a bad case of the lover's nut." No one was around, but he was talking out loud just the same. It was a habit he had developed while he rode a tractor long hours in the field. "God damn. I need me some sex."

He had only driven about five miles when he decided to take the shortcut through the old Wayne Place where a dirt road diagonally connected two highways that ran almost perpendicular to each other toward town. The short cut intersected the main road at Blythe and would get him home a few minutes earlier.

"I need some music," Willis said and turned the radio back on. This time he found a gospel station playing *"What a Friend We Have in Jesus"* and turned the volume up on high and sang the lyrics at the top of his lungs. When he reached Piper's Pond, he pulled over to the side of the road and reached under the seat where he kept a pint of Jim Beam hidden. This one was a new pint. He had bought it earlier in the day on the way to Augusta when he had run an errand for the boss. He unscrewed the top and gulped down half of it. He replaced the cap, wiped his mouth on his sleeve, and put the liquor back under the seat.

"I'm gonna get some sex tonight," he sang to the tune of *"What a Friend We Have In Jesus"* as the liquor warmed his gut and lubricated his brain with vulgar thoughts. "I'm gonna get some sex tonight," he sang as he pulled back onto the road. He hoped Annie wouldn't have a headache, or he'd have to force her.

155

Just before he reached the intersection at Blythe, Willis saw a flash of red along the roadside. He rubbed his eyes and looked again. It was a young girl in bare feet in a red tiered skirt and peasant blouse. "This is my lucky night," Willis said. "My lucky night." He pulled up alongside the girl and offered her a ride.

"No, sir. I'll just walk, thank you," she said in a high scared voice.

"Get in the car. You don't need to be walking these roads at night."

"No, sir. I'm just fine. I don't need a ride."

Willis stopped the truck and got out. The girl, sensing trouble, started running. It didn't take Willis but a second or two to catch her.

"Where you going?" His crotch was on fire.

"Leave me alone. Let me loose!" she was screaming. "Please let me loose!"

Willis clutched her tightly and dragged her back to the truck. She was no match for him. His rugged strength and determination made short work of his intentions. "Give me some pussy, bitch," he said.

"Please, sir! No! No!" she was screaming.

Willis held on to her with one arm and lowered the tail gate to his truck with the other. When it was down, he thrust her up into the truck bed and began ripping her clothes off.

"Please quit! Please! No! No!" her screams continued.

The sand on the bed of the pickup drew blood from the young girl's backside as Willis pulled her toward him. He pulled her legs apart on the tailgate where they dangled off the end and then unzipped his pants.

"No! No!" she was shouting as he entered her. "Somebody help me!"

It was over quickly. Willis grabbed her torn dress and wiped his limp penis with it before zipping his pants back up. "Get off the truck, bitch," he said. "I'm going home."

The young girl lay there whimpering. Blood was smeared between her legs and visible on her tan thighs. "Somebody help me," she was still screaming.

"I said get off," Willis ordered. When the girl didn't move, he grabbed her by the legs and pulled her off the truck onto the road where she fell in a heap crying.

"Stupid bitch," Willis said to her. "Shouldn't be walking alone on the road at night. You deserved it." He pulled the pint bottle out from under the seat and gulped down the rest of it before getting back into the truck and driving off toward home.

Fifteen minutes later Annie heard Willis' truck come in the driveway. It had a loose muffler and he liked to race the engine just before he cut it off.

"Amy, set the table, your daddy's home." She walked over to the stove and stirred the pot of salmon soup. He might be hungrier than usual tonight, she thought, I better thin supper out so there'll be enough for everybody. She picked up the water pitcher, walked over to the stove, and added a quart of water into the pot, then shook pepper and salt into it quickly before he came in the door.

Willis smelled the salmon soup as soon as he opened the door. "God damn it, Annie. Are we eating that shit again tonight?" He slammed the door behind him, causing the calendar to fall off of the wall. She noticed the date when she picked it up and hung it back on the nail in the wall. There were four days left before pay day.

Annie lowered her eyes and turned around to face him. He's been drinking, she thought. I can smell it on him. "It's all we have, Willis, until payday. I don't have any more money for groceries. You didn't give me any last week. I had to break open the children's piggy banks and borrow money from them so we could eat tonight." She looked up and glanced over at him to see how he was reacting to her comments and noticed the red blood stain on his pants beneath the zipper. "Willis, did you hurt yourself? You're bleeding down ..." Annie glanced around to see if the children were close. "You're bleeding down there."

Willis looked down at his crotch. "Oh, shit. I cut myself today. I didn't know I had bled on myself down ... there." He left the room and headed for the bedroom. "I better change clothes," he thought.

He stripped down to his drawers and noticed blood on them as well, so he took them off and wadded them up in his blood-stained pants. "I'll rinse these off myself," he thought and threw them in the bottom of the closet. All of a sudden he felt dizzy. He steadied himself and grabbed a pair of boxer shorts folded on the floor before sitting down on the side of the bed. "I think I'll just take a short nap," he thought after he put them on. He passed out before his head hit the pillow.

When Willis didn't come back into the kitchen for supper, Annie sent Amy to find him. The other children were already seated at the table.

"Willis is asleep," Amy said when she returned and sat down at the table.

"Let's give thanks to the Lord for our supper," Annie said, and they bowed their heads in silent prayer. Annie prayed for food for her children. The little children didn't pretend to pray and began to eat.

Amy did pray. She prayed Willis would die so their lives would change for the better like the people she read about in magazines. She prayed he would suffer while he died like he made them suffer.

After the kitchen was cleaned and the children were in bed, Annie went into the living room to read. She went to the makeshift bookshelf – a long, unpainted board held up by two concrete blocks – and picked up her tattered Bible and carried it to her chair.

The tears came silently and flowed down her cheeks. She wiped them away with her sleeves and willed them to stop, but they kept coming. "I wish he was dead," she thought.

Willis was up and out of the house early the next morning. It was Friday and payday. His head hurt, and he knew he should wash out the back of the truck in case the girl reported the rape to the police. "They ain't gonna git me," he thought. "I'll say she came on to me. Asked for it. Hell, she begged for it. Wanted it. They all do."

Annie heard him leave but acted as if she were sleeping. She didn't want to chance an argument with him. Early morning arguments were the worst with him. Mornings were when he said the most hurtful things to her after the children left for school.

"Where'd you be if'n it weren't for me," he'd say. "Working in some flop house with that brat of yours. That's where you'd be. Look at 'ya. You look like a scarecrow. Nobody would have you. Hell, I wouldn't have you now, but it's too late. We're married." He'd harangue her until he left for work and often continue the argument when he returned home in the evening. His behavior always made the children cry, and Amy would rush them to their rooms and read them a story until Willis tired of berating her.

On this day, after the children left for school, she fed the baby and put him back to bed. She felt weak and hoped it was from all the crying she'd done the night before. "Maybe a sponge bath would make me feel better," she thought.

She went into the kitchen and placed a pot of water on the stove to heat. She then went outside to the rain barrel and brought in a large bucket of water which she placed inside the tub.

As she undressed, she looked at her image in the mirror. She was rail thin. Every rib protruded and her breasts were almost non-existent. "Annie, you're a mess," she said out loud. "What happened to you?" She laughed at her own question and said aloud again, "Life happened. Life and wrong choices."

When the water heated on the stove, she brought it into the bathroom and poured it into the bucket and sponged herself clean then soaked her feet in the lukewarm water for a while. When the water cooled, she toweled herself off and put on fresh clothes. "Lord," she said out loud, "I hope you will forgive me for wishing Willis dead, but I do wish it. I wish it more than anything."

A voice in the back of her head reminded her that, if Willis were dead, she would have no money at all instead of a little money every now and then. She grabbed a broom and began sweeping the sand out of the house.

By the time the children were home from school, Annie had bathed the baby and placed him back in his crib where he played happily. Amy helped the other children with homework and then went into her bedroom to read.

Annie baked some biscuits to go with the leftover salmon soup and set the table for supper. The pleasant day ended when Willis came in drunk.

"We havin' that same old shit for supper again?" he said.

"Willis, it's all we got."

"All you got ... all you got ..." Willis said in a falsetto voice. "All you got ain't enough." He reached over and grabbed Amy by the arm. "Now this one ... this one's more like it."

Annie recognized the lecherous look on his face. He was all but drooling. "Willis, if you lay a

163

hand on her, I'll kill you. I'll kill you," she was screaming now. "I'll kill you so fast you won't know what hit you."

Willis was laughing. "You ain't doing nothing to me. If there's one thing that don't scare me, it's you."

Amy left the room and took the children with her. The baby had started to cry.

Now alone in the kitchen with Annie, Willis pushed her out of her chair on to the floor and said, "Don't you dare threaten me in front of our children again, bitch, or I'll kill you. I'll slit your throat and place you in a creek full of moccasins." Willis knew she was afraid of snakes.

Annie pulled herself off the floor, and Willis hit her. Hard. He hit her so hard she fell against the window and broke it. One of the glass shards stuck into her arm and she began to bleed profusely.

"Now look what you've done, you stupid bitch, broke the window and we have to pay for it. I'll tell you one thing ..." he walked over to her.

Annie's head hurt but she had had enough. She wasn't going to give him another chance to hit her. She grabbed a wrought-iron frying pan from a nail on the wall and swung it toward Willis.

It connected and Willis fell to the floor. In a blind rage Annie hit him again and again and again.

She stopped when Amy came into the room, shook her, and took the frying pan away from her. "Momma, stop. He's hurt bad. Don't hit him anymore."

"I don't care, Amy," she said. "I hope he is dead." She dropped down on her knees and began to cry. "I pray to God he's dead. I pray to sweet Jesus he's dead. I want him to be dead."

It was not to be. Willis began to whimper and moan and they knew he was still somehow alive.

"What are we going to do, Momma?" Amy said. "There's no telling what Willis is going to do to you now."

"I don't care," Annie said. "There is nothing he can do to me now that he hasn't already done." She paused and said, "Go get a blanket, Amy."

"A blanket?"

"Yes, a blanket. We are going to put a garbage bag under his head and wrap him in a blanket to keep him from bleeding all over the place."

165

"Then what?"

"I don't know. I'll have to think about it," Annie said.

Amy helped Annie off the floor into a chair and began to clean the blood spatter in the kitchen. Blood was everywhere: on the walls ... on the ceiling ... and on Annie. Willis's head was covered in blood and his face was turning purple. One eye was hanging out of its socket.

When Amy returned with the blanket, Annie already had Willis's head lying on top of a garbage bag. They slid the garbage bag and Willis over on to the blanket and rolled him up in it.

"What about your arm, Momma? It's bleeding too."

"Don't worry about my arm. Just tie a rag around the cut and it'll be all right. We need to clean the floor," Annie said and grabbed a towel.

Amy tied a rag around her mother's arm and went to the rain barrel for water. They worked until the kitchen was cleaned, then dragged Willis out to the porch, down the steps, and somehow lifted him up to the bed of his pickup truck.

"What are you going to do now, Momma?" Amy said.

"Don't you worry about it. Just take care of the children until I get back and don't say nothing to nobody. If the children ask, just tell them something. Anything. Anything but the truth." She opened the door and was glad to see Willis had left the keys in the ignition.

"I know they heard y'all fighting, Momma, but they were sleeping when I went in to get the blanket."

Annie closed her eyes and took a deep breath. "Amy, it would be better if they don't know their daddy and I are gone. If they wake up and ask, just say anything you have to say to get them back to sleep. Okay?"

"Okay, Momma."

Willis moaned loudly as Annie turned on the truck, and then he was silent. "It's the first time he's ever passed out for a good reason," she thought.

Amy stayed awake as long as she could but eventually fell asleep. When she awakened the next day, her mother was home and asleep. The truck and Willis were gone.

167

Later in the morning, while the children were playing outside, Amy said, "What'd you do with him, Momma?"

"You don't need to know. Everyone will know where he is soon enough. The less you know, the better off you are and maybe me, too."

It was a long day. Amy and Annie looked at each other often but neither spoke.

The sun was setting when they saw a plume of dust rising above the corn field along the road to the house. It was a county sheriff's car. They sat still until he knocked on the front door.

"Come in," Annie said.

The door opened and a young deputy sheriff walked in, hat in hand. "Ma'am, I have some bad news for you."

"Bad news?" Amy sat down in her chair.

"Yes, ma'am. We found your husband's body this afternoon."

"His body?"

"Yes, ma'am. He had only been dead a few hours when we found him. Somebody beat him up pretty bad."

Amy said, "Somebody beat him up? Do you know who did it?"

The young deputy glanced over at Amy and said, "No. We don't know. We thought we had a lead, but the man has an alibi."

"Man?" Annie said.

"Yes, a man." The young deputy noticed neither Annie nor Amy seemed to be grieving over the news about Willis, nor did they look at each other. Both were now silent.

Annie finally said, "Where was he?"

"Parked behind the old barn on the abandoned Harper property."

"Was he drunk?"

"We think so, ma'am, there was a strong smell of whiskey in his truck. He was lying outside of it. Funny thing is, ... no other tire tracks were around at all." The deputy scratched his forehead, then said, "No footprints, either. He was parked in the grass."

Annie began crying. It was from relief, but the deputy thought the news of her husband's death had finally sunk in. "So sorry, ma'am."

"I understand, deputy, it's just so sudden. Who do you think did it?"

"Who do we think killed him?"

"Yes. The man you said had an alibi."

"You don't need to know that, ma'am. It was just a man that was mighty mad at your husband. Said he'd ..." the deputy paused and turned red in the face. "Said your husband had molested his daughter Thursday night." He took a step forward, sighed heavily, and said, "It was just an accusation, ma'am. That's all it was and ..."

"He was home on Thursday night," Annie said interrupting the deputy.

"I'm just telling you what the man told us, ma'am."

"Willis did come in later than usual, though, Momma," Amy said.

"He did?" The deputy stepped back and looked squarely at Amy.

"Yes. He'd been drinking then, too," Amy added, "and he was in one of his mean moods."

The deputy took out a note pad and wrote something down and said, "What time did he leave today?"

"I'm not sure. He was gone when I got up. He was drinking last night, too," Annie said.

"What about you, miss? Did you see him this morning?"

"No, sir," Amy said, "he was gone when I got up too.

A door slammed. Little Harry yelled out, "My daddy was mad last night. He was yelling at my Momma. They was fighting."

"That true, ma'am? Were y'all fighting?"

"Yes. We did have a fight, but that wasn't unusual when was he drinking. He was a surly drunk."

"Don't say my Daddy's a drunk. You made him that way. He told me so himself," said Little Harry. His face was a portrait of pure hatred directed at his mother. As the old-timers like to say he was his daddy made over.

Annie shook her head and began crying again. Amy walked over and took her hand. "Don't cry, Momma. It'll be all right. We'll get along some way."

The deputy called Little Harry over to him and said, "Did you see your Daddy leave today?"

"No. He was gone when I got up. He was gone all day. He likes to fish on Saturday. I reckon

171

he was fishing. Sometimes he stays gone. He'll be back late tonight, I betcha."

The deputy now knew Little Harry hadn't heard the news of his father's death. He wasn't going to be the one to tell him, so he said, "Well, I reckon that's all I need from y'all. We'll keep you informed of our inquiries." He tipped his hat and left.

"What was that cop doing here?" Little Harry said. He still had a belligerent tone in his voice.

Annie was silent for a moment, then said, "Harry come over here and sit by me. I have something sad to tell you."

By the next morning, news of Willis's death had spread, and a couple of people came by the house to express their condolences. The deputy also reappeared. "He died from blunt force trauma," he said, "but that's about all we know. We got no leads at all. This case may never be solved, ma'am. I'm sorry about that." He also suggested Annie contact a funeral home to take the body after the county coroner released it.

Amy read to the children most of the day and, except for Little Harry, who was despondent, everyone was quiet. Late in the afternoon, Annie went to her bedroom, shut the door, and knelt by the side of her bed. "Oh, God, I wish I was sorry Willis is dead, but I'm not. I know I'll be going to hell, but I need to ask you one last thing." She crossed herself and sat down on the floor. "I don't have any money to bury him, God. I don't know what to do. I need your help, Lord." She sat there with tears rolling down her face, staring into space until the baby started crying. It was only then she knew it was supper time, and food was scarce. The salmon stew was gone, and only a couple of uncooked potatoes remained in the kitchen along with some stale crackers and an unopened box of chocolate-covered cherries she'd hidden in the pantry since Christmas.

Shortly after the children were in bed, there was a knock on the door. Amy was in the front room reading, so she answered the door. It was Willis's boss, Sheffield Herndon.

"Evening, miss," he said. "Is your mother here?"

"Yes, sir, I'll go get her." Amy walked quickly to the kitchen where Annie was washing dishes.

"Mom, there's a man here to see you. It's Willis's boss, Mr. Herndon."

173

Annie dried her hands on a rag and went to the front room. She had never met Willis's boss before, but she had heard he was an ogre and hard to get along with, according to Willis.

He was a short man, nicely dressed, and was carrying a brief case. As Annie entered the room, he said, "Good evening, Mrs. Smith. As you know, your husband Willis was employed by me."

Annie's expression didn't change. "Yes, sir, that's what he told us."

"May I sit down?" Mr. Herndon said.

"Oh, I'm sorry, I wasn't thinking." Annie pointed to a chair in the corner and said, "Please sit down."

"Fine. I will," he said and sat in the chair, then opened his briefcase on his lap.

"Mrs. Smith, I know you have had it hard up to now. Willis didn't make much money, but he did have an insurance policy."

Annie's eyes opened so wide she could have been a cat on catnip. "An insurance policy? How'd he pay for it?"

"I paid for it." Mr. Herndon said. "I have policies on all my employees in case of an accident, and Willis was no different." He reached into the briefcase, pulled out a manila envelope, and handed it to her. "All of the details are there. The policy is paid up, so you just need to contact the people at the number listed in there, and they will see that you get what's coming to you."

"I don't know what to say, Mr. Herndon." Annie sat opposite Mr. Herndon holding the manila envelope without opening it.

"There's no need to say anything. Your husband's dead, and I know you're going to need all the help you can get." He shut the briefcase and stood up.

"I don't know what to say," Annie said again. "Thank you, Mr. Herndon. This will help us out more than you know."

"It isn't a lot, Mrs. Smith, but I suspect it'll get you on your feet until you figure out what to do."

Mr. Herndon walked to the door and said, "Again, Mrs. Smith, I'm sorry about your husband." He opened the door and left.

Amy had been sitting in the room silently. Now that she and her mother were alone, she said, "What's in the envelope, Momma? Maybe we'll get five thousand dollars. Maybe we'll get ten thousand dollars." Amy's face was all smiles.

"I doubt that it's much," Annie said, "but it will be enough to bury him. Maybe there'll be enough left over for us to leave here and go somewhere else."

Amy walked over to her mother, "Well, go ahead, Momma, open it. Open it."

Annie handed the envelope to Amy. "You open it. You read better than me."

Amy took the envelope and went over to the chair in the corner near a lamp. She took the papers out and spread them on her lap. She looked at the first page, then the second, and then the third.

"Oh, Lord, Momma, it's twenty-five thousand dollars. We're getting twenty-five thousand dollars." Amy jumped up and began to dance around the room.

"Twenty-five thousand dollars? Are you sure?" Annie stood up and walked over to Amy. "Are you sure?"

"Yes, Momma, I'm sure. Look at this paper."

Amy looked, and the amount on the paper was twenty-five thousand dollars. A rare smile spread across her face.

"Oh, Amy," she said, "this means we can leave here and go somewhere new. We can find a nicer place to live. One with running water and schools nearby."

The smile on Annie's face disappeared. "But first we have to bury Willis."

"How're you going to do that, Momma?" Amy said.

"I'm going to have him cremated."

"You're going to burn him up?"

"Yes. I'm going to burn him up."

"What about his ashes?"

"We'll worry about that later. I'm sure we'll figure out something to do with 'em."

Amy shrugged and said, "If you say so. I'd just throw them in the field if it was me."

"Let's call it a night, Amy. I'm tired, and we have a lot to do tomorrow."

"I know. We have to find a phone, too," Amy said.

"Lots to do," Annie said and went to her room.

She knelt beside her bed. "Thank you, God. I don't deserve the money for what I did, but it'll help the children. I hope you understand." She prayed for the children and, as an afterthought, prayed for Willis, too. Then she crawled into her bed and had a good night's sleep for the first time in many years.

She was safe.

Hurt Feelings

Like the song says: If it weren't for bad luck, she might not have had any luck at all. Aunt Sallie Mae's lifelong grief began when she was born the youngest of four children to an absent father, and a mother who liked sailors a lot. It was downhill from there. She cried all the time, and her mother often left her in the care of her older siblings.

Aunt Sallie Mae married Uncle Joe at sixteen, had four children in four years, and was an old woman rocking on the front porch by the time she was twenty. She still cried as much as she did as an infant.

Her misfortune wasn't due to an early marriage or the uninterrupted string of births; it was because she was shy, gullible, and tenderhearted. Her siblings teased her from the beginning. They teased her unmercifully until she was dead and in the ground. Instead of talking of her good deeds at her wake, family members were holding their sides with laughter over jokes played on her during her lifetime.

"Remember when Sam told everyone she was adopted?" someone said.

"Yep. She worried about it always, but not as much as she worried about what we did with Joe's body when we took him out of the casket and hid him." (Our family has wakes at home to honor the dead, so the brothers found it easy to remove the body and sit it in a chair reading a *Playboy* magazine in the garage.) Thank God she didn't find the body. They returned Uncle Joe to the casket when she wasn't looking. I don't know what they did with the *Playboy* magazine; I suppose they put it inside the casket too.

The laughter was broken up by yet another mourner who said, "The best joke played on Sallie Mae was when Harry asked her to keep his pets. Remember?"

I don't know much about the early teasing because I wasn't around. I do remember things her younger brother Harry said and did to her – especially the pet story. By the time everyone had passed on, except for Harry, she had begun calling me when she was distressed.

I believe the pet incident happened in the summer because it was exactly one year after Harry's only son died tragically. (Harry was headed to Atlanta to court his widowed daughter-in-law which is another story in itself.) Aunt Sallie Mae called and said, "Little Kay, your uncle is mad at me, and I don't know what to do."

Her crying over Harry's antics was normal, but I said, "Why's he mad, Aunt Sallie Mae?"

"I won't keep his pets."

"You won't keep his pets? What pets?"

"Harry says they are his favorite ones and can't be left alone. I can't keep them. I just can't," she said between sobs and hiccups. "He says he's going to tell everyone I hate pets." She was becoming hysterical. "I don't hate pets. I just can't keep his pets here."

When the story was finally told, here's what must have happened. (I'm sure Harry had had too much to drink; his drinking is legendary in our family.) Harry in his inebriated state decided to take up the family sport, called Sallie Mae on the phone, and said, "Sister, I'm going to Atlanta for the weekend, and I need you to keep my chickens for me."

"Chickens? You want me to keep chickens for you?" (I'm sure Aunt Sallie Mae asked about the chickens twice, because no one in their right mind would think they heard that question right the first time.)

"Yep, Sallie Mae. I said chickens," he said. "Prize-winning, game chickens. Handsome chickens. Bantams. The kind that Daddy used to raise. In fact, a couple of them are probably kin to daddy's chickens." That statement was tantamount to consecrating the chickens with holy water. Anything close to their daddy was saintly in Sallie Mae's eyes and had to be given special consideration – even chickens.

She must have paused for a moment before she said, "Harry, I can't keep them, honey. I don't have a fenced yard." Bear in mind Aunt Sallie Mae would have kept the chickens in her yard if her yard were fenced to please her brother. She loved him dearly.

"Fenced yard? You think I'd keep these fine chickens in a fenced yard?" Harry said.

At this point in the conversation, I know Aunt Sallie Mae must have backed away from the phone shaking her head in disbelief. The "fine chicken and no fence" statement would put any country person off. Any farmer, fake or real, knows that keeping chickens in a fenced area is preferable if only to protect them from predators – and a fence is a "must have" to keep people from tracking chicken poop into the main house.

Since he probably wasn't getting a quick answer from her, Uncle Harry surely repeated himself. "Sallie Mae, did you hear me? I need you to keep my chickens this weekend, and they can't stay in a fenced yard."

"Well, I guess I could keep them on the porch, Harry."

"Porch? You think my chickens would stay on a porch? Fat chance of that. These are house chickens, Sallie Mae. House chickens. You've got to keep them in the house."

It took all of her courage, but she said "no" to Uncle Harry's chicken request and hung up the phone crying. She was afraid she'd hurt his feelings.

As for Harry, he hung up the phone laughing, because he'd just pulled another fast one on her and caused her to cry. He didn't have any chickens. It was a joke. The kind they played on Aunt Sallie Mae all of her life.

I sent flowers to her funeral. She was ninety-four when she died. "Make the bouquet the prettiest you can. A big one on a stand," I said to the florist. He promised he would create a special arrangement - something to commemorate her longevity and love of the South.

Shortly after the funeral my mother said, "Kay, those flowers you sent were the ugliest flowers I've ever seen. Why in the world did you send them?" She laughed in her special way that always made me wince and be glad I had on clean underwear.

To make matters worse, she was right. The flowers were ugly. I was afraid I'd inherited Aunt

Sallie Mae's bad luck when I saw them: There was one magnificent magnolia blossom in the center, but the other flowers looked like they'd been sitting in a pot on someone's porch and neglected for years. I shook my head and stared at my mother who spoke the truth and didn't have a tender bone in her body. The truth was a sword with her; she'd stab it right in you whether you wanted to hear it or not.

That's the moment I understood Aunt Sallie Mae's tenderness, and how much her feelings were hurt when someone caused her pain for no reason. I wish I'd understood it earlier and applied it to my life. That was my bad luck – and the reason I now bite my tongue whenever I'm tempted to say something evil.

To anyone I may have upset in the past, I apologize. Everyone else can rest assured they are now safe from insensitive jokes from me. There's no dirt on the high road, and I'm taking it.

Homeless

I should have known it was going to be a memorable day when I dropped the puppy on its head at eight o'clock one morning. I was outside getting the newspaper when it happened. I couldn't hold on to the squirming puppy, and he fell. He began to cry pitifully after hitting the sidewalk.

I panicked, picked him up, ran into the house, and called the vet. "Bring him in right away," the vet said.

I threw on my cleanest dirty clothes, grabbed some shoes, and ran from the house holding the still squealing puppy. We raced to the vet's office.

We arrived twenty minutes later. The puppy was no longer crying, but I was. "Please get the doctor," I said quietly to the receptionist. "I dropped the puppy on its head."

"You did what?"

I thought she might be partially deaf, so I loudly said, "I dropped the puppy on its head. The vet needs to check him right away."

The receptionist stood up and slowly walked to the back. She came back a couple of minutes later with the vet in tow. "She dropped her puppy on its head," she said and pointed to me. The room had filled up with other patients, and they all turned and stared at me.

I was compelled to say, "I didn't mean to do it. It was an accident." I clutched the puppy close to my heart.

The vet took the puppy from me and said, "Wait here. I'll check him in the back."

When I sat down, the people on either side of me moved to another area of the waiting room. I stared straight ahead to avoid their dirty looks. They were certain a puppy abuser was in their midst.

It was such a hostile environment that I was afraid someone would call the police and I'd be arrested. I envisioned the newspaper headline underneath my mug shot, "Animal Abuser Drops Puppy on Its Head."

My nightmare lessened when the vet brought the puppy back. He had good news. "He's okay. Puppies are very resilient. He might have a little headache, so keep him as quiet as you can today."

I nodded, paid the bill, and headed back to my house. Two blocks down the street, I felt a familiar rumbling in my stomach; I knew I should visit a bathroom soon. "No problem," I thought. "I can drop by my shop and use the one there."

I drove to the shop, got out of the car, and went to unlock the door before I realized I didn't have the key with me. The bathroom urgency was growing more extreme, so I phoned my friend Martha who lived close by.

"Martha," I said. "I forgot my key, and I need to borrow your bathroom. May I come by?"

"Of course," she said. "Come on."

Four minutes later I was at Martha's house and solved my urgent problem. As I walked back to the car, Martha said, "Good Lord, what happened to you this morning?" She had a startled look on her face.

I laughed and said, "Do I look like a homeless person? I need to go home and change."

"You don't have time to change," Martha said. "It's ten minutes to ten and you have to open the store."

"Oh my God," I said. "Can you open it for me this morning, Martha? I don't want to go to work looking like this."

"Sorry. I have a doctor's appointment. Otherwise I'd be happy to help you out."

I must have looked forlorn, because she added, "You look okay. Just go on to work with what you have on."

"Oh, Martha," I said. "I can't go to work looking like a homeless person."

"You don't look much like a homeless person," she said and laughed. When she saw my reaction to her statement, she added, "I'm just kidding. You look fine. Go on to work and don't worry about how you look."

I did. It was a good day, even though one customer asked why I had on one black shoe and one brown shoe. "Color blind," I said to avoid telling her I'd dropped a puppy on its head.

At the end of the day, I packed up several needlepoint projects in a large grocery bag. Strings from the canvas edges were hanging out of the top, but I ignored them. On impulse I grabbed a roll of toilet tissue and placed it in the top of the bag. "Never know when I might need it," I said out loud to myself.

I put the puppy in his carrying case and placed the other two poodles on leashes. I picked up the bag of projects to be finished, along with my pocketbook and walked out the door and locked it.

As we crossed the street, one of the poodles pulled his collar off and headed into traffic. He barely missed being hit by a speeding, city bus and several cars.

I was terrified. I had turned to stone and couldn't move. After dropping one puppy on its head in the morning, I had just avoided having another pet killed in the evening.

Luckily, a homeless man on a bicycle across the street grabbed him and yelled, "I've got him, Miss."

"Thank you so much," I said. My heart was racing. I checked for traffic and crossed the street clutching the encased puppy and my pocketbook in one hand and holding the grocery bag and the poodles on leashes in the other hand. I was no longer worried about the mismatched shoes.

"Hand me the collar, and I'll put it back on him," the homeless man said.

"No. I'll do it. Just hold him for me." I put the puppy in his case down at my feet and sat the grocery bag beside it. Just then, a city bus came barreling by at an ungodly speed sending a gust of air toward us. The blast of air quickly knocked over the grocery bag. The needlework items stayed put, but sent the toilet tissue spiraling into the street.

I was mortified. A moment before no one but me and the homeless guy were on the street. Now hordes of tourists were walking by, but none gamely offered to retrieve my runaway toilet tissue. The homeless man was silent on the subject, yet he looked at me knowingly. So, much to my embarrassment, I walked into the street and retrieved the toilet tissue.

The homeless man held onto the runaway poodle and, as I placed the collar back on the dog, the homeless man said, "These sure are pretty dogs. How do you keep them looking so good living on the street?"

I blushed and could think of nothing to say, so I said, "It isn't easy."

He smiled broadly and said, "Find somewhere warm to sleep and have a good night."

I smiled and waved goodbye as he bicycled away and thought, "I am going to kill Martha."

I saw the homeless man numerous times throughout the winter and he always waved and asked if I had had a good night's sleep.

"Sure did. And you?" I would reply.

Seeing him was a memory trigger for me because thereafter, I'd always look down at my shoes to make sure they were the same color.

Good Intentions

People say B Poole could climb a tree in his bare feet. I never saw him do it, but there are people in Burke County where he lived who swear by it; they say he did it on a regular basis while working for the forestry service. They also say he knew where every stolen car or dead body was hidden in the county. Some he reported; others he didn't. I don't know the answer to that either. I guess he thought some people needed killing. He did say that to me one time.

What I do know is he was a sharecropper and claimed to be a Coonass Cajun from Louisiana. He was also a hard-working and kind man. No one ever told me how he ended up in Georgia, and I never asked.

The first time I met B I was struck by his height and his resemblance to the picture of Abraham Lincoln that hung on a wall in every school room I ever entered. He wore overalls – sometimes with a shirt and sometimes not – and no shoes except on Sunday when he attended church at what he called the "First Holy Ghost Hollerin' House Mission." I don't know if they played with snakes or not, and I don't believe that was the name of his church even though he claimed it was true.

The Pooles lived in an unpainted, vintage house with rotting screen doors and broken out windows just down the road from me. It was a Southern, shotgun-style house with a center hall and four rooms downstairs and four up. (A shotgun-style house is one where you can shoot a gun through the front door and the bullets go straight through the back door without hitting anything.) A porch surrounded the house on all sides. It must have been a handsome house when first built, because it still retained a hint of its former splendor. The wainscoting and deep crown moldings were a glimpse into the magnitude of the lives of those who'd lived there before B. It was never meant to be a sharecropper's residence, but it suited the Pooles.

We formed a friendship since B and his wife were my only neighbors for miles around. I lived nearby with my first ex-husband who was a gentleman farmer with little proclivity for communication with women. He was emotionally unavailable to me, and I don't know if I ever pleased him; I still wonder about it sometimes. That's the main reason I fell into step with B and his wife. They taught me how to can food, make pickles, and clean fish, although I preferred to have them delivered as if they were straight from the grocery store. Once B discovered my preference, he never brought unscaled fish to me again; they were always ready to "fry up," as he liked to say.

At other times of the year he brought berries, vegetables, and the occasional piece of deer meat, which was odd because B loved deer. There was one living in his house along with a raccoon and two possums when I knew him. Mrs. Poole never commented on the situation, so I assume she loved animals as much as he did. As many times as I

197

visited them, I never smelled any foul odors or sensed their home was unclean in any way.

It was a welcoming house but not well-furnished. Several pairs of old Irish curtains hung over the windows in the front parlor on the left side. There was a tired sofa with mismatched cushions and two wooden chairs facing each other in front of the fireplace. There wasn't a rug on the floor, but a magazine rack next to the fireplace sat atop a gray bathroom mat. I don't know what was in the room on the other side of the hall since the door was always closed, as was the door into the room behind the living room. I suspect they were empty. The remaining door led to the kitchen, which was the only room in the house with any color. It was painted a bright yellow everywhere – walls, floor, ceiling, windows, table, chairs – everything except the refrigerator, which was a sickening avocado green, and the cast-iron, wood-burning stove, which was black except for the rust around the edges. I guess you could say the stove was well-loved and in good condition for its age. I never went upstairs, so I don't know what was there at all, but there must have been a bed.

I spent lots of time in the Pooles' yellow kitchen after I had my first child. With no one to talk to at home, I found myself driving down to their place often. My young son was excited to see Happy – the deer B kept in the house as well as the raccoon, possums, birds, and other creatures that shared the home. Invariably other injured animals would appear and disappear after they had healed. I don't know where B learned to heal them, but he had the magic knowledge to perform miracle cures.

Aside from the mammals he nursed back to health, he'd bring in injured birds with broken wings. I saw my first eagle and many varieties of hawks up close with B. They would never screech. They seemed to know they were in good hands. He'd wire their wing together until it healed, and if there was an open sore, he'd cleanse it with some type liquid before plucking a few of the bird's feathers and covering its open wound with them.

The creatures came in broken and confused and left looking for happiness as if they had just been given a dose of amphetamines. He was glad to see them go. Not that they were a burden to him in any way. He loved them. He was just pleased to have space for another injured spirit. "When one flies out – another can fly in," he'd say. "I can fix anything but an injured spirit. That's something the Lord has to take care of." He'd pause and then add, "I mean the Lord gives us all the opportunity to find the strength to heal ourselves, don't he, Alice?"

I once asked B if any of the creatures he nursed back to health ever came back. "No," he said. "Animals and birds don't dwell on the past. They look to the future."

B and his wife must have sensed my unhappiness, but they never said anything to me about it. They came by to see me more often if I stayed away when the "blues" crept in and as my marriage deteriorated.

The year I left, I had a two-year-old daughter and a four-year-old son, both at the bright-eyed age when everything in life is a puzzle waiting to be solved. B helped my son learn to clean fish that spring, after which he took a fish completely apart. He said he was trying to figure out what made fish swim. My mother-in-law said he might be a budding serial killer because of the fish dissection. I didn't respond to her concern, but it gave me a glimpse into why my husband never had much to say.

One beautiful summer morning my son and I went down to visit B and found him with a young raccoon riding on his shoulder. "Follow me," B said and led us to a nearby tree. He reached up and pulled down a branch. We could see a bird's nest hidden in the leaves with two babies cheeping at us. I watched my son's eyes widen as the babies lifted their beaks, expecting to be fed. Suddenly the raccoon swept down, grabbed one of the baby birds and gobbled it up before hopping off B's shoulder and heading toward the woods with a fast, ambling gait. I was convinced my son would be scarred for life because of this murderous incident, but he clapped his hands, looked up at me and said, "Momma, did you see the coon eat that bird?"

My son wasn't traumatized, but I was. B said, "Don't be upset, Alice. Children accept how things are with nature. It's us, the adults, that don't. We ignore reality and pretend a different outcome can be had if we do things differently. Children aren't hindered by the ignorance of maturity." Today he might say we spend too much time being politically correct. I suppose we do.

I thought about what B said later that day and into the weeks that followed. I spoke to B and his wife often, but by fall I knew I would be leaving. I could no longer ignore the broken bonds of my marriage. My husband had grown more distant and was seeing another woman, although I was unaware of it when I left; I'm glad I didn't know. Apparently he didn't know he had to stop dating when we married.

I regret I didn't keep up with the Pooles more often after I left. I'd see them sporadically at the grocery store, which was twenty miles away from where they lived, and running into each other was always coincidental. I'd begun working for a newspaper and wrote a weekly column which they read religiously. They told me how much they enjoyed it each time we met. I appreciated their support and told them so but not often enough.

B was right about the ignorance of maturity. I believed the Pooles would be around forever and postponed going to visit them because there was always tomorrow. I had good intentions.

I wish I could thank B and his wife for taking me in when my spirit was broken and I needed healing. I flew away healed and searching for happiness just like the other injured animals that appeared on their door steps.

Strom Thurmond's Tea Party

Mrs. Thurmond was dying. She was sitting in a squeaky Lincoln rocker on the back porch fanning herself while staring vacantly at the kittens playing on the porch steps. Even when she stood up, her once tall frame was now stooped, and she seemed two feet shorter than she had years earlier. At ninety, her mind wandered in and out, confusing everyone as to where she was at any particular time. Sometimes she was thirteen again. At other times she was on vacation in Italy. Every now and then she would regain her senses and recognize somebody, although she usually didn't remember anybody's name. Today was different.

"Betsy," she said to her daughter, how are you, my dear? Have you had a face lift?"

"Alice, you're looking good. You must have a new man in your life?"

"What have you two been up to? No good, I'll bet."

Betsy and I, friends for over fifty years, always answered her questions good-naturedly, even making up answers we thought she would like when we didn't know the real answers. We sometimes gave her answers she'd like even when we knew the right answer.

"Who's president now?"

"Strom Thurmond."

"Strom? That's wonderful. Do you remember the tea party I had for him when he was running for president?" Strom Thurmond had been her late husband's brother.

"Yep. Sure do." I said all the while thinking, *"Remember when you threw us in the yard and said we couldn't stick our fingers into the petit fours? Remember when you said we were too little to go to a big people's part?. Remember when you said little girls in South Carolina should ..."*

"Where's my Spottie Dog? Have you seen Spottie? He acted so strange at the party. I've always wondered what made him act that way."

Betsy and I stared at each other contritely. We knew exactly what had happened to Spottie Dog on that beautiful sunny day. We had kept our guilty secret for over fifty years.

Strom Thurmond was running for president as a Dixiecrat candidate, and there was a tea party at Mrs. Thurmond's house. It was hot. It was so hot everyone in Aiken County was walking around in as few clothes as they could without being arrested for indecent exposure. I was invited over to participate in the event, not as a party-goer, but as a companion for Betsy.

The tea party was scheduled for four o'clock in the afternoon. By one o'clock in the afternoon, the kitchen was full of helpers making tiny sandwiches. Loaves of white bread were stacked on the counter and one helper was cutting off the crusts while another took a cookie cutter and cut out little rounds of white bread; the rounds were then covered with mayonnaise and topped with a slice of cucumber or tomato. Another helper was polishing silver at the

207

sink, while still another was complaining that the cream cheese was still too solid to mix up with mayonnaise and black olive or pineapple pieces. This mixture was also spread on the little rounds of bread. All of the trays of sandwiches were covered with moistened towels to keep the bread soft. Boxes of chocolate candy were kept in the refrigerator, so they wouldn't melt from the heat before serving.

Best of all, there were boxes and boxes of sweets from the local bakery. Petit Fours with decorations of pink roses on top, bourbon cookies laden with pecan chips, chocolate-covered pecans, and cakes. And there were lots of cakes: They were to be sliced just before the guests began arriving.

Betsy and I hung around the kitchen for a long while until someone noticed us eating cheese straws and picking the icing off a cake. Mrs. Thurmond was summoned and we were quickly relegated to the yard with Spottie Dog. It was too hot to stand in the sun, so we sought out a favorite hiding spot under the rose bush on the right-hand side of the house and waited for the party-goers to arrive. It seemed to take forever.

Finally, the first car pulled up. It was a huge black Cadillac sedan. Strom and his first wife Jean got out. We wanted to run out and greet them, but remembered Mrs. Thurmond's warning not to bother the guests and stayed safely hidden.

"Look at her hat, Betsy. It's huge. Huge and black," I said.

"Yeah. Dummy. It's black because she wants it to match her shoes," Betsy said.

"She isn't matching her ugly shoes. She's wearing it because she has to wear a hat to a tea party. And white gloves, too."

Another car pulled up and then another. And another. We stopped our squabbling and stared at the procession of women in hats and gloves. Hats…hats…hats. We had never seen as many hats.

When the last car was parked, and everyone safely inside, we began to sulk.

Spottie Dog was sulking, too. He just hung around with his tail between his legs and looked sad as if he were hoping someone would report us to the police for tying him to the rose bush.

"It's not fair. Why do we have to stay out here?" Betsy said.

"Old people are just mean, that's why. Don't you know anything about old people?" I said.

209

We felt slighted, and the longer we stayed under the rose bush the more mistreated we felt. We were unwanted. Unloved. Almost orphans.

"I'd let my children come to my party," Betsy said.

"Me, too. I'd even let them eat all the food they wanted. I'd even invite Spottie. I'd never make him stay outside," I remember saying.

We were miserable. We were rejected. We were political prisoners. And within minutes we began plotting revenge.

Neither Betsy nor I remember whose idea it was to let Spottie go to the party in spite of the admonitions against it. Betsy remembers it was my idea; I remember it was hers. Regardless, we were determined to prepare Spottie for the party.

We crept out from under the rose bush and carefully walked around the house staying close to the foundation bricks, and crawled under the windows so no grown-ups could see us. When we were sure nobody was looking, we ran across the yard to the garage and found the bicycle pump. One of us held Spottie Dog fast, the other inserted the bicycle pump nozzle in his rear end, and began pumping him up. Spottie Dog wiggled and tried to get away, but we held fast and kept pumping.

When Spottie Dog was full of air, we sneaked back around the house, carried him up the steps to the front porch, opened the door, turned him loose, and ran to the front window to peer in and see what happened. We didn't have to wait long.

Spottie Dog ran and farted his way throughout the house, searching for his mistress Mrs. Thurmond.

Some of the ladies held their noses, trying not to look embarrassed – nobody talked about farting in those days. Others acted as if nothing was happening and continued holding teacups with their pinkies in the air. We looked carefully around the room, but we couldn't see what Strom was doing.

By this time we were laughing so hard we abandoned our plan to remain undetected. We knocked over one of the porch rockers causing Mrs. Thurmond to head for the porch and the source of the commotion.

We saw her coming and ran to hide under the rose bush once again. Betsy scratched her arm on a thorn and wiped the blood on her shirt; I scraped my knee, but other than those mishaps, we returned to our clandestine spot safely.

Mrs. Thurmond knew exactly where we were hiding. "Do you girls know what is wrong with Spottie Dog?"

We didn't dare tell her the truth on that long ago day, but today was different. She was ready for the truth and we told her.

"You rascals. I should have known," she said and laughed out loud.

She was quiet for a moment, then said, "Where's my Spottie Dog?" She had left us again to visit some other place in her memory bank, but we finally had a clear conscience. We had been absolved of any feeling of guilt over Spottie Dog's behavior at Strom Thurmond's Tea Party.

Bunica's Gift

My name is Edie Macrae, and I was born too soon to be a flower child and too late to be a baby boomer. By the time women were burning their bras and celebrating the birth control pill, I was married with two children of my own.

Sometimes I look back to the sixties and remember how different things were and who I was in those days. Every female I knew was examining her life, seeking her inner self, or discovering who she was meant to be. I was too busy keeping house, changing diapers, fixing meals, and performing other domestic activities to do much of anything except be a wife, mother, and daily problem-solver. Even so, I remember daydreaming of a different life ... one like my husband's cousin Cerise had in California where she went to work daily. Her husband was a lawyer, and they had a live-in nanny who stayed home and took care of their child.

If the truth were known, the feminist movement was well underway before I even knew there was one. Everywhere I went – to church, to a social gathering, or to the grocery store - my friends were flexing their feminist opinions to their husbands and other men hoping that someone would take them seriously. I never joined in. I didn't know where I stood on any subject, unless it was about getting diapers and my husband's shirts a bright white when they were washed. I can actually remember worrying about my husband's "ring-around-the collar" status, whereas today, I'd tell him to wash his own shirt if it bothered him. But times were different then, and I was still living in an unaltered state of bliss.

When I married John, women were wearing hats and gloves. By the time our second child arrived, women were burning their bras and practicing free love. American culture seemed to have changed in the blink of an eye. Those from a larger city might read this and wonder why behavior in the sixties and seventies seemed strange, but for a girl from Savannah, Georgia, whose travel log included shopping at Rich's in Atlanta and crossing the state line into South Carolina to buy firecrackers, the options of free sex, marijuana, and going braless were enough to give even a Savannah prostitute the vapors in those days.

I do remember looking into the mirror often and staring for a few seconds before asking myself, "Who are you?" The mirror never answered back, and I always walked away wishing I knew who I was for certain as I went back to my world of diapers, dinners, and debutantes.

My routine never changed, and when my husband announced we were taking a trip to the West Coast to visit his great-grandmother, I was excited. I had never been to the West Coast or practically anywhere else, for that matter.

John made sure we had a babysitter. He said, "Edie, we can act like we're on our second honeymoon."

I said, "You've got to be kidding. You might get lucky, but not if you act like you did on our first honeymoon."

215

Alice Twiggs Vantrease

My smart-alecky comment didn't faze him at all. He ignored it. I promised myself if he ever took umbrage at one of my sarcastic remarks, it would mean he was actually listening to something I said.

We arrived in San Francisco just after noon on a Friday in October 1969 and in plenty of time to check into our hotel before taking in the sights. On Saturday we were scheduled to visit with my husband's great-grandmother Bunica. She came to America from Romania just before the dawn of the twentieth century and was 100 years old. Her birthday and age were the reasons we were making the trip because it might be the last time we could visit her before she croaked.

Bunica came to America as a young girl through Ellis Island. She immigrated from Carei, a small Romanian town near the Hungarian border. No one is sure how she ended up in California, but it must have been because of her husband, who was also Romanian. He sharpened knives and scissors for pennies a piece off of a cart and eventually opened a hardware store and catered to the rich and infamous from the waterfront to Nob Hill. It was the American

Dream for them, just as it was for hundreds of thousands of other immigrants of the era, but he was long dead and never discussed to my knowledge. He must have left a decent estate because their children were well-educated, and Bunica didn't depend on the kindness of anyone. She was quite independent financially and in other ways, I'd heard.

John was an only child on his side of the family, so any information I gathered about his family was limited to what he could remember and the tales his grandmother had shared with him about Bunica.

"Some of the younger people in our family think Bunica is a gypsy," he said one day out of the blue.

"A gypsy? Why?" I laughed out loud. "Aside from the fact she looks like a gypsy in the picture in your study."

John's blue eyes crinkled, and he said, "Just because she is dressed in black, has a kerchief on her head, and a black shawl around her shoulders," he paused and shook his head and said "... surely that's no clue. She's stooped over." He leaned toward me menacingly and said, "She has gnarly fingers." John was laughing as he continued to expand his description of Bunica. He was still laughing when he sat down on the edge of the bed.

When he caught his breath, he was silent for a few moments, and the smile disappeared from his face. He was strangely somber and said, "I don't know why they think she has gypsy roots. She's a Romanian Jew. Jews aren't gypsies. She doesn't say much to anyone. She always sits in a special chair in the corner of her drawing room; it's decorated just as it was when she moved into the house decades and decades ago."

I suddenly had visions of crocheted doilies along the backs of chairs to keep the gentlemen's pomade from slicking up the furniture. I wondered if she had a black cat named Basarab or Onyx that sat by the fire. I also wondered if she had a crystal ball and long, painted fingernails.

"Does she ever tell anyone's fortune?"

"No. Not that I know of," John said. "She never says much of anything. Nothing at all."

"She doesn't say anything at all?"

"Well, what I mean is she doesn't carry on a conversation. She just sort of takes it all in. She watches people." John scratched his ear. "I used to think she could see straight through me and everyone else in the room. She'll speak her mind if she thinks something ought to be said."

Although I had never met her, Bunica always sent cards and gifts to us and remembered every important event and date for family members. My husband hadn't seen her but a couple of times since he'd been an adult. "The first time I remember meeting Bunica," he said, "she hauled me out of the dining room by my ear and made me eat in the backyard because I was chewing food with my mouth open."

"You're kidding. She did that the first time you ever met her?"

"Yep. Said if I was going to eat like a pig I could sit in the yard where the pigs would eat - if she had any. Then she began speaking in her native tongue. I guess it was Romanian because I didn't understand a word she was saying, but my mother followed us out and explained it to me after Bunica went back into the house. I was about six years old."

"Wow. How'd that make you feel?"

"Great! Bunica lived on top of a hill, and I could see over the roofs of the other houses and had a grand view of San Francisco Bay. I loved it." John leaned back and gave one of his great big belly laughs that I loved to hear. Then he was quiet again, and his eyes grew all misty.

I didn't interrupt his thoughts because I knew that visit was the last time he ever saw his parents. They died shortly thereafter in an automobile accident. His grandmother raised him, but she was gone now too. She was Bunica's daughter. Bunica had outlived them all.

We hadn't been in the hotel ten minutes before the phone rang. I shook my head *no* since we were already amorous and had our clothes half off. John was about to get lucky.

He answered the phone anyway. "Yes?" A wide grin spread across his face. "Cerise, how'd you know we were already here?" He walked over to the window and stopped midway when he ran out of cord. "You're amazing. I can't wait to hear more about the job." He laughed again. "Dinner sounds great. What's the address?" He waved at me wildly and motioned for a pen. I shrugged my shoulders.

"Just a minute, Cerise. Let me find a pen." John opened the drawer to the nightstand, rummaged through it, and pulled out a pen.

"Okay, what's the address?" He was scratching down information so fast that I hoped we could decipher it later.

"No. Nothing's changed. She's the same old Edie. She'll never change."

I wanted to slap the crap out of him, but I went into the bathroom and slammed the door instead. And, yes, I stared in the mirror and asked myself, "Who are you? Are *you* amazing?" The mirror, of course, said nothing. I was beginning to feel as if it might be a long weekend.

John finally hung up the phone, knocked cautiously on the bathroom door, and said, "Cerise wants us to join them for dinner. I told her we would. We're meeting them in Chinatown. She said it was something you really ought to take in while you are in San Francisco since it's your first trip here."

"Okay with me, but right now I think I'll take a nap," I said as I walked out of the bathroom and got into the bed.

"Want me to take one with you?" John said and gave me a lecherous look.

"No. The time difference is getting to me. I really do need a nap."

He left me alone, and I must have fallen asleep right away. When I woke up it was twilight, and John was fast asleep in the chair across from the bed.

The clock on the bed side said six o'clock. John hadn't said a specific time when we were to meet Cerise, so I got out of bed and walked quietly over to him and kissed his cheek.

He was startled. "Jesus, Edie. You scared the shit out of me."

I backed away from him and said, "What time are we meeting Cerise and Mr. Cerise for dinner?"

"Seven."

"It's after six now, so you'd better get moving."

John took a quick shower, and I pulled out my little black dinner dress. It was perfect for just about any occasion at home, and I decided to wear my pearls. I hoped I would look sophisticated.

We arrived at the restaurant ahead of Cerise and her husband, so we went into the bar to wait. I decided to live dangerously and ordered a dirty martini with extra olives. By the time our dinner dates arrived, I was very relaxed.

John made introductions all around, but Cerise only had eyes for him. She was all over my husband like a cheap suit. I had to ask her husband twice what his name was, because it was so loud in the bar; Cerise hadn't bothered to introduce us. His name was Ed.

Cerise was dressed like a gypsy with a long skirt and lots of beads. Her hair was long and hung straight down her shoulders to her waist. I thought her hoop earrings were too big, and I was certain she was wearing too many bracelets.

Ed and I made polite talk during dinner as John and Cerise entertained each other. I thought Cerise would never shut up. She yakked and yakked and yakked about her job and about important meetings and solving employee problems in a brilliant way. I interrupted several times to ask about her son, but she waved me off saying, "I'll get to him in a minute."

We never did "get to him," and when Cerise asked if we'd like to go down to the wharf for one last drink, I kicked John under the table. He ignored me.

I kicked him again to no avail. I finally said loudly, "I am really tired. We are still on East Coast time, and I need to get my beauty rest."

"Certainly, dear," Cerise said, "some people need more help than others. It's good that you are aware of your limitations." She then laughed too loudly at what I hoped she meant as a joke.

It took me a minute before I realized I had just been insulted. I felt a flush creep over me from my toes to my nose. My eyes narrowed to slits as I said, "John, it's time for us to call it a night."

John ignored me, presumably because he was picking up the tab. Cerise was leaning across the table, giving him a full view of her breasts which were almost falling out of her top. Ed was staring at a Chinese figurine beside a fish tank, and I was about to explode. My head was throbbing at the base of my neck, and I felt my temples pulsing.

"John, did you hear me? It's time for us to call it a night."

He came out of his trance and looked at me. It was as if he had suddenly realized other people were in the room. "What did you say, Edie? You want to go back to the hotel?"

"Yes. I think we should call it a night."

John stared at me with a look that would have been intense, if he hadn't had too much to drink. "Well, okay. If that's what you want."

Then like a snake sensing a weakened prey, Cerise struck. "Surely you're not calling it a night, John. Don't be such a country bumpkin. The night is still young. There are plenty of places we can go for a nightcap."

The "country bumpkin" comment sealed it for Cerise. John said, "Let me call you a cab, Edie. Since you're tired, you can go on back to the hotel. I'll be along later."

Ed was still imitating a clam, and any hope he would take a stand on ending the evening was moot. He had been tamed.

"No, John," I said. "We are both going to call it a night." I was tapping my foot and holding my own hand to keep from slugging him.

I leaned over and whispered in his ear, "If you don't leave right now with me, I am going to slap your cousin as hard as I can." He finally got the message. We came straight back to the hotel.

I was glad to crawl between the sheets, and John fell asleep quickly. I stayed awake thinking about Cerise and women working and what in the hell I was good for other than housework and a cheap lay. I remembered to take two aspirins because I didn't want a hangover.

We woke up early, and John got lucky. It was only four o'clock in the morning in San Francisco. We had breakfast, showered, and made ready for the day.

We arrived at Bunica's house a few minutes early. The front door was open. John let us in and steered me to the right into a large, dark green parlor. Bunica sat in a corner chair. She looked the same as she did in the picture in John's study. We waited for her to say something, but she just sat there and looked at us. John finally walked over and gave her a peck on the cheek. "It's good to see you, Bunica," he said.

Bunica looked over at me and said, "So this is Edie?"

John motioned me over, and just as I came close, Bunica said, "Pull up a chair, John. Pull one up for Edie too. I want to learn what you've been up to since I last saw you."

John pulled a chair over, and I sat down. Bunica was quiet afterward, so I just sat there and imitated a statue with her.

It wasn't long before Cerise and family arrived along with several other relatives and their entourage. The house was teeming with people of all ages, but none as old as Bunica.

Cerise was holding court in her la-de-dah way, and I watched and listened as people told her how smart and beautiful she was. Today she was wearing a navy suit with a white silk shirt and stiletto heels. Her hair was in a bun, and she wore gold jewelry. I was glad I had worn a suit too, although I had on flats. Bunica still said nothing, so I kept silent too.

About thirty minutes into the event, Cerise's husband instructed their little boy – he was about six years old – to go over and give Bunica a kiss.

"No. I hate her," the child said loudly. Everyone in the room stood still and stared at him.

Cerise and her husband took the little boy outside. When they returned, there was another request to the child. This time louder and more commanding, "Go over and give Bunica a kiss. It's her birthday."

227

The child walked slowly over to Bunica, kicked her in the shin, and said, "I hate you."

The parents grabbed him and took him outside again.

Bunica had not made a sound. She shook her head and said, "That's what happens when a child has no direction. The father doesn't know how to function as the mother. The mother doesn't know who she is, so she takes a job to find herself, and the child is left to run wild."

She adjusted her scarf and pointed a gnarly finger at herself. "I always knew who I was. I was the cook. The gardener. The maid. The laundry woman. The seamstress. The chauffer. The nurse. The teacher. I was everything in my family. I always knew who I was."

She looked into my eyes to see if I understood her. It was as if she had x-rayed my soul and knew everything I was feeling.

"Bunica, thank you," I said and gave her a hug. She was startled but smiled at my unexpected embrace and pushed me away.

We celebrated her birthday with cake and ice cream and, after a long nap, caught the "red eye" home. It was a good trip.

Bunica died the next year, and as I look back upon the trip to San Francisco, I realize how important she was in helping me understand my life's worth. I no longer look into the mirror for answers. My life was and is far beyond the sum of its ordinary parts.

I am Edie Macrae, and in my own life and in my own way, I am amazing.

The Stump Preacher

It was almost sunup, and Old George was already on his stump preaching. "I like to get up with the Lord and fill up with the Holy Spirit," he said, if asked.

George Williams was an elderly black man who lived with his daughter in a cabin in the woods behind the Rucker Street school house. He was almost blind and had been preaching on the stump for as long as anyone could remember.

George, now gray-haired and stooped with age, was once a tall man. Nature had been kind to him, and regardless of the vegetables laden with fatback, fried meats, and desserts filled with flour and sugar, he never gained weight and maintained his lithe frame with ease. If asked, he said that he only wore solid black suits with a white shirt and black string tie.

No one challenged him on the color issue, since they knew he was almost blind and saw everything in black or white. Old George actually wore suits of different colors. Red ones ... blue ones ... green ones ... purple ones; they all looked the same to old George. No one had ever seen him in anything other than the colorful suits, except when he went out calling and put on his formal beaver-skinned top hat.

On occasion, someone with good intentions would give him a pin-striped, hand-me-down suit, or a plaid flannel shirt. George always thanked the person profusely then gave the clothes to a good friend or other person in need. He was almost blind, but he could still see stripes and plaids and believed the Lord frowned on such frivolity. Friends gave him the colored suits but always cautioned others "don't tell him no different" because they knew how he felt about black and white. Therefore George preached from the stump every day clad in a colorful suit with matching suspenders and white ruffled shirt.

When he first began to preach, people came from miles around to see what he was wearing on a given day, but he had been preaching for so long that he had become part of the scenery. As he grew older, few people took the time to drive by and marvel at his outfits.

Every now and then, someone would get up early and check to see if he was up and preaching. He always was; no one could say they had ever beaten him to the stump.

Jane and Joe Rollins, ten-year-old twins who lived nearby, tried repeatedly to get up at dawn and race to the stump but invariably failed. Sleeping late was a curse thrust on them by a bevy of kinfolk who also embraced the habit of arising late in the morning. Plus, it was summer and there was no school to attend.

On this particular day, Joe awakened early and tip-toed across the hall to Jane's room where he carefully opened the door and crept to the side of her bed. "Jane," he whispered, "Jane. Wake up. It's almost sunup."

Jane stirred a moment then turned over and said, "Shut up, Joe. Can't you see I'm sleeping?"

233

Joe pursed his lips and leaned back for a moment. Thinking long and hard before doing anything was a long-term habit of his. When he had thought about it long enough, he reached over and pinched Jane on her backside.

"Ouch," she said too loud.

"Sh-h-h-h-h-h," Joe whispered, "Someone will hear us." He leaned close to her ear and said, "Get up. If you stay in bed any longer, we can't beat Old George to the stump."

At this reminder, Jane sat up in the bed, rubbed her eyes and said, "Then get dressed, Joe. I'll meet you downstairs in a minute."

When Jane and Joe dressed alike, no-one could tell them apart until they were close enough to see their eyes. Jane's eyes were blue; Joe's were green. Both wore their hair cropped short, and Jane prided herself on being a tomboy and just as tough as Joe. On this particular morning they did not deliberate on what to wear, but they dressed alike just the same. Both wore blue jeans and white shirts. They knew better than to wear anything else. The fact that Old George was usually resplendent in a colorful suit didn't matter to them; they knew he was a preacher and was allowed such affectations. They also knew he only saw things in black and white.

"The Lord likes things black and white," Old George said. "Good or bad. Happy or sad. The Lord don't like no thing done half ways. No gray. No sorta good or sorta bad. No sorta happy or sorta sad. It's like being dead … you either is or you ain't," he explained to them when they wore colorful plaid shirts to hear him preach the first time.

They first heard about Old George when somebody at school called them over to the back wall at the school yard. They could hear someone hollering out the scriptures. They climbed up on the wall and peered over. They saw an old man standing up on a stump, arms outstretched, beseeching the wicked to reconcile with the Lord.

Somebody in the group said, "Old George knows the Bible frontwards and backwards." Jane and Joe were suspicious of the claim. They were taking confirmation classes at church and having a tough time memorizing the names of the books of the Bible.

It didn't take long for the twins to decide to go meet Old George. They walked over to his house one day after school and found him preaching loud and hard to the air and animals surrounding him. An old, blue-tick hound lay at the base of the stump and two calico cats lay nearby. None were awake or appeared disturbed by his yelling. They were used to it.

When Old George sensed that someone was nearby, he stopped preaching, wiped his brow with a white handkerchief, and stepped off the stump. "Who's there? What you doing here?" he said.

Jane and Joe didn't say anything. They were frozen in position and couldn't quit staring at Old George. His eyes were wide open and blood shot; his nostrils flared like a bull before a matador. He was dressed in a neon purple suit, and his shirt had ruffles at the sleeves.

Old George stepped closer to them until he could see their shapes and said, "Well, speak up. What you chillun' doing here? You ready to be born again. Ready to trust in the Lord?"

As he walked closer, the twins stepped backward. Joe finally said, "We heard you know the Bible backwards and forward. Is it true?"

Old George rolled his eyes at heaven and said, "You got your Bible with you?" He didn't look right at them, he seemed to look over their heads as if searching for a missing halo. Jane thought he might be looking right through them. One eye sort of rolled to the right, and she couldn't tell for sure where it was looking.

Joe, who was digging in the dirt with the toe of his left shoe, looked down at the ground and said, "No, sir. We have a Bible,. but we didn't bring it with us." Jane was quiet. She was wishing she had worn a dress instead of blue jeans and a shirt. For the first time in her life she wasn't sure if being a tomboy was a good idea or not.

Old George stared them down for a long minute, then said, "Why you interested in the Bible? You go to church?"

"Yes, sir," Jane said. "We're trying to learn the books of the Bible so we can be confirmed."

"That's right," Joe said lamely. "We're trying to memorize them, but it's hard."

Old George wiped the sweat off his brow again before waving them off with handkerchief. "Y'all come back when you have your Bible." He turned around and climbed back on the stump yelling, "The Lord is in his holy temple, the Lord's throne is in heaven: his eyes behold, his eyelids try, the children of men. The Lord tryeth the righteous..."

His voice trailed off as the twins climbed back over the wall and raced across the school yard towards home.

It would be days before they made the trip back over the wall. When they did come back, Old George admonished them for being late and reminded them that the Lord liked early risers and that was why the early bird got the worm.

After that, the twins began to wonder if Old George ever stopped preaching; they vowed to beat him to the stump one morning just to see if he ever slept. Their curiosity was in charge on this morning when Joe woke Jane up before dawn.

When they met in the kitchen. Joe said, "Don't forget the Bible."

"I've got it," Jane said, and they scurried out the door.

Cotton puffs of fog hung over the landscape as they began their walk. A lone whippoorwill called out as if to herald the day instead of its usual celebration of the night. It was "first light" as the old folks called it, and the twins could only see indeterminate shapes in front of them. It would be another half an hour before they could see anything clearly.

"Let's take the long way around so we can stay on the sidewalk," Jane whispered.

"No. It'll be quicker if we cut through the schoolyard," Joe said.

"I know," Jane whispered again, "but it's scary. I'd rather go on the sidewalk."

"Why are you whispering, Jane?"

"Just am. Don't want to wake anybody up."

"We aren't going to wake anybody up. They're all still in bed." Joe said loudly as if to prove his point.

"Not everybody," their next-door-neighbor called out to them. "Some of us are up early to enjoy the sunrise."

Jane and Joe shared guilty looks and said, "Mornin'," at the same time and continued their trek.

"You don't think she'll tell on us, do you?" Jane said.

"Nope."

"You sure?"

"Yep."

"How sure?" Jane wasn't convinced that the neighbor would keep quiet.

"Very sure. She isn't speaking to Momma right now." Joe said and kicked a pebble down the sidewalk.

When they reached the school yard, Joe turned and walked through the gate into the schoolyard while Jane continued down the sidewalk. The fog puffs had lifted off of the ground and were raised a foot or two above the soil and grass, thus blurring the landscape more than before. Joe quickly disappeared into the mist, and Jane panicked when she turned around and couldn't see him.

She stood there quietly and felt her heart begin to race. An owl hooted in the distance, and a nearby dog bayed. The hair on the back of her neck stood up.

"Joe," she whispered, "I can't see you. Where are you?"

When there was no answer, she said, "Joe. Where are you? Joe?" Her voice was louder now although quavering a bit from fear.

Joe heard her clearly and wasn't going to answer, but changed his mind when he heard her call out again.

"Joe, I'm scared. Where are you?"

"Inside the schoolyard, Jane. Are you coming with me or are you going to stay on the sidewalk?"

"I want to stay on the sidewalk."

"Well, I'm not." Joe said. "I'm taking the shortcut."

There was more silence for a few seconds while Joe sat on a swing set waiting on Jane to find him.

As Jane turned around and walked back down the sidewalk to the schoolyard gate, she felt something brush against her and screamed, "Help. Joe. Something's trying to get me."

The "something" was one of Old George's calico cats looking for a rub from a friendly human, and Joe was quick to point it out when he reached her.

"Jeez, Jane, it's just a cat. I thought you weren't scared of cats."

"I'm not. I just didn't know what it was in the dark."

The cat rubbed up against her again, and Jane reached down and scratched its neck. The cat's purr was amplified in the fog, and when Jane and Joe left, it followed them across the schoolyard to the wall that separated the school from Old George's stump. The cat leapt ahead of them and scrambled over the wall before they reached it. They didn't hear any preaching. It was still dark and quiet.

"I think we're going to be up before him this time," Joe said and giggled.

Just as they reached the wall, they heard a door slam. A few seconds later Old George began preaching, having stopped long enough to get a biscuit from the kitchen.

The twins looked at each other in disgust. Joe shook his head and said, "We're too late...again."

They waited for a moment and then climbed up the wall. When they reached the top, Joe called out, "Mr. George, it's us – Joe and Jane. We've come to hear you preach."

Old George stopped and looked over in the direction of the wall. He couldn't see them, but he recognized their voices. "Y'all bring your Bible with 'ya?"

"Yes, sir," Jane said. She pulled it from under her arm and held it out to him as if he could see it, although she knew he couldn't.

"Have you been working on the names of the Bible books?" Old George said.

"Yes," Joe said.

"Yes, sir," Jane said.

"Well then, let's hear them. Both of you together...the first one is..."

"Genesis..." Joe and Jane said in unison.

"And then comes...," Old George said.

"Exodus, Leviticus, Numbers, Deuteronomy, Joshua, Judges, Ruth..." The twins stopped to catch their breath and pull their memory together before continuing again.

"Then comes First Kings," Joe said.

"No, it's not," Jane said. "Next comes First Samuel, then Second Samuel...then First Kings and Second Kings."

Joe joined in and the twins called out the names until they reached Lamentations and stopped their recitation.

Old George, seated now on the stump, looked over at them and said, "Well...what's next?"

When Joe and Jane couldn't continue, he finished for them...ending with Revelation. Old George breathed a sigh of satisfaction and said,

"There. There are sixty-six books to remember. Only sixty-six. If I can remember them and can't see nothing, how come y'all can't learn 'em when you can see everything?"

Joe felt his ego plummet. He knew he hadn't studied as hard and long as he should, yet couldn't bring himself to admit it. "We study as best we can, Mr. George, but we are just learning them. You've known them a long time."

Old George chuckled and nodded at them. "Yes. I've known them a long time. A very long time." He rubbed his pant leg and straightened its seam between his fingers then said, "They was called out to me. Each and every one. Called out to me by my grandmomma. She learned them from her mother 'fore she taught them to me."

"You never learned to read?" Jane said.

"No. Couldn't see. Besides, even if I could've it wouldn't have made no difference. School was for readin' other kinds of books and doing numbers and such." He turned his head from side to side and said, "My grandmom learned me everything I know. If it weren't for her, I wouldn't trust in the Lord and be able to preach his word."

"Did she teach you the words to the Bible too," Joe said.

"Yes, she did. Taught it to me from beginning to end. Each and every word. Everything that's in the good book she taught me."

Joe turned around and looked at Jane before staring back at Old George. "So it's true," Joe said.

"Is what true?" Old George wrinkled his brow, and Joe and Jane both thought they saw him stare directly at them, except for the one eye that wandered around. But a few seconds later, both eyes were focused together and staring over their heads.

"Is it true that you know the Bible backwards and forwards?" Joe said. He had his arms crossed and was staring straight at Old George.

"Yeah," Jane said with her hands on her hips, "We heard you know the Bible backwards and forwards. We heard you know everything that's in it." She had a daring tone to her voice.

Old George recognized doubt when he heard it. He cocked his head to one side and said, "Is the sun up, yet?"

"Yes, sir. It's up," Jane said.

"Well, then. You have your Bible. You can read. Why don't you test me. Call out a number from a verse and chapter in the Bible. Test me on whether I can remember it."

Joe looked sternly at Jane and said, "We believe you. We don't have to test you." He was feeling guilty about questioning the old man.

As Jane opened her mouth to argue with him, Joe clamped his hand over her mouth. She wanted to say that she didn't believe anyone could know the Bible backwards and forward and all the way through, but didn't.

Old George knew they were evading the truth so he said, "Hand me your Bible." He reached out for it but stayed seated on the stump.

Joe hesitated, then took the Bible from Jane and gave it to Old George. Old George closed his eyes and opened the book. He pointed to place in the middle of the right hand page and said, "What am I pointing to?"

Joe reached over and took the Bible back and saw that Old George had pointed to Jeremiah, Chapter Two, Verse Six.

"Well, what is it?" Old George said.

"You pointed to Jeremiah," Joe said, "Verse Six of Chapter Two."

Old George said, "Just a minute, I've got to step over here behind the hedge and get my thoughts together." He walked behind the hedge covered with honeysuckle vine and reappeared thirty seconds later. "Sometimes I need to step aside and fill up with the Holy Spirit," he said.

Old George sat down and leaned back on the stump. He thought long and hard before reciting: *"Neither said they, Where is the LORD that brought us up out of the land of Egypt, that led us through the wilderness, through a land of deserts and of pits, through a land of drought, and of the shadow of death, through a land that no man passed through, and where no man dwelt?"*

Joe and Jane were reading the words as Old George recited them. They looked at each other in amazement.

"How'd you do that?" Jane said.

"Yeah, how'd you do it?" Joe said.

Old George chuckled. "I been knowin/ them words all my life." He reached out his arm and said, "Call out another test for me. I want you to be sure I be knowin' the good book. You pick it this time."

247

Jane faced Joe and said, "Okay, Joe. You turn to a page and point out a verse."

When Joe picked out a verse, Jane said, "He picked out The Book of Ruth, Chapter Four, Verse Seventeen."

Old George scratched his head and said, "Now that's where they talk about all the begetting. Let me see now..." Jane and Joe knew he was thinking hard and long through his memory bank in order to come up with the right words. All of a sudden he laughed out loud. "Aha. I got it. *And the women her neighbors gave it a name, saying, There is a son born to Naomi; and they called his name Obed: he is the father of Jesse, the father of David.'* That's right, ain't it?"

"Yes sir, that's right." Jane said.

"We best be going," Joe added. "Our mom will be looking all over the place for us."

As the children stood up to leave, Old George said, "When you come back, make sure you know all the names of the books in the Bible. All sixty-six of them. You hear me?"

As Joe and Jane climbed back over the fence, he began preaching again in a quiet voice. He was seated on the stump, but they knew by mid-afternoon he would be hollering out verses of the scripture to anyone passing by or to the birds in the trees. It didn't matter which to him. They were all God's children. Seemed to him that the more he preached, the more the birds sang in the mornings, as if they too were thankful for another day. He depended on the Holy Spirit to keep him preaching no matter what.

The twins spent two hours a day for the rest of July with Old George at the stump. He praised them when they remembered the Bible books in the correct order and chastised them when they forgot. Regardless, by the end of the month, both children had the books memorized.

On the first day of August, Joe and Jane walked back over to meet Old George. They didn't come back at dawn this time; they waited until after breakfast. He was on the stump preaching as usual. His voice was full of energy and he was warning passersby to stay clear of the money lenders.

Old George knew they were there before they said anything. "How come y'all are late?" he said.

"We practiced calling out the names of the Bible books before we came. We know them by heart now," Joe said.

"Well, let's hear them," Old George commanded.

Jane and Joe went through the list without mistake and Old George gave them each a quarter. "If you learn them backwards before school starts," he said, "I'll give you five dollars apiece."

He laughed and clapped his hands together. "My grandmomma was right. If you learn the Bible, it will show you the way to a good life. She paid me two dollars for learning the books backwards."

By the end of the summer, the twins had learned the names of the books backwards, and one late August morning they made the trek over to Old George's so they could collect on the bet.

When they got there, he was gone. There was no smoke coming from the chimney, and the blue tick hound and calico cats were nowhere around. As they turned to leave, a car drove up, and his daughter got out of the car and walked toward them. "You here to see George?" she said.

"Yes, ma'am. Is he here?"

"No. George passed three days ago. We buried him yesterday afternoon, but before he died he said to find you children and to give you something."

She reached in her bag and took out two, crisp five-dollar bills. She handed one to Joe and one to Jane and said, "He said for you to always remember the names of those books – forwards and backwards." She paused and leaned down so she could look them straight in the eye. "He also said you were good children and would always remember what was in those books. You are good children, right?"

Jane and Joe were too teary to respond so they mumbled 'thank you' and headed home. It would be thirty years before the twins went back to the place where Old George preached.

The weathered stump still sat in the same place, but the hedge covered with honeysuckle vine was gone and the house had been moved several hundred feet back into a meadow to make way for the widening of the road. A large bulldozer was leveling the land, and they were there when it pushed Old George's stump over and shoved it to the side of the road along other debris that was already on fire.

The bulldozer moved toward them and the twins stepped back as it stopped. The driver, covered with a fine mist of dirt, stepped out of the cab and walked over to them. "Can I help you with something?" he said.

Joe was the first to speak. "No. We just came by because we used to spend time here when we were children. There was an old preacher who lived here. He used to preach from that stump you just pushed over."

"No kidding," the man said.

"He was filled with the Holy Spirit," said Jane.

"He was full of spirits, no doubt about that," the man said. "You should have seen what we turned up behind the hedge when we bulldozed it down."

"Yeah? What was behind it," Joe said.

"Must have been an eight-foot high stack of half-pint bottles of rot gut whiskey. All of it covered with honeysuckle vine. No telling how long it'd been there." The driver grinned, and the twins noticed how crooked his teeth were. "Think that whiskey might have given your preacher some inspiration?" he said.

"Guess so," Joe said.

As they walked away, Jane said, "Revelation..."

"Jude," Joe answered.

"John, three, two and one, and Peter two and one," Jane said.

"James, Hebrew, Philemon, Titus..." Joe said.

When they finished reciting the books backwards, Jane could have sworn she heard Old George say, *"Now go on home and have a little helping of the Holy Spirit and enjoy the rest of your day."*

Perspective Changes

The African-Americans of my childhood were good to me. I loved visiting them and spent many hours in their cabins eating cookies, collards, or grits, and listening to stories they'd tell. I was oblivious to their living conditions; their homes seemed warm and inviting and often more welcoming than my own.

Our family lived in an old house in the country. It was the remnant of an old plantation house, one of two houses built for twin sons. Ours survived the Civil War because the gardeners moved into it after the white folks left; the other house was burned by the Yankees.

We had lots of help - all black: Jesse Bell was our nanny; Catherine Gardener, whose family took the last name of their profession after the Civil War, lived in a small house adjacent to our property and did our cooking and cleaning; and Lily Twiggs did our laundry and ironing. Jim Turner was a handyman around the place and was too old to do much of anything, but our family took care of him anyway. Jim lived on our place in an old cabin at the edge of a pecan grove with his wife Zerelda; she had been born in New York and didn't remember when she first came to the South.

Jim Turner was born the son of slaves. No one knew how he ended up at our place; He didn't remember either, since he'd been there so long.

Lily lived in a cabin across the road from the back of our property and had the same last name as ours. She was also the daughter of slaves, and her family took the Twiggs name after the war ended. No one explained that fact to me as a child; I believed her to be kinfolk. The difference in skin color wasn't important: she loved me, and I loved her.

As a country child, I didn't understand the significance of race relations because we had a symbiotic relationship with everyone around us. They depended on us, and we depended on them. Our black nanny lived with us and took care of us. Our cook was as attached to the land as we were to ours; her family had lived next door for well over 100 years

It wasn't as if we were privileged – we weren't. It was a different time, and we were far removed from the acrimonious race relations we often see today. The African-Americans in my childhood had class distinctions: colored people were decent folks; those identified by the "N" word were thought to be black trash synonymous with white trash. Everyone wasn't dumped into the same cultural or societal bag - white or black.

When I started school, I was exposed to other friends and environments. I remember being shocked that colored people were not allowed to drink out of the same water fountain and had to enter through a separate door. I instinctively knew it was wrong.

It made me feel guilty when I went anywhere with my beloved nanny Jesse Bell and she was treated differently. She would always lower her eyes when we went places, as if she was shy. Now I know it was because she was uncomfortable. She had to enter any doctor's office through a door marked 'Negroes' -- if she could find one.

I was just as surprised to discover many white people made "colored folks" use special glasses, plates, and utensils. It was as if one might change skin color just by using the same eating tools. I thought it ridiculous, but to my enduring shame I never questioned it.

Several years ago I had the opportunity to go back and visit these haunts of my youth. I don't know what I was expecting, but it wasn't what I found.

Catherine Gardner's house was the same as it had always been in my memory. It was still painted mint green with "haint blue" shutters. It was a voodoo color of blue renowned for keeping out ghosts, Boo-Daddy's, Boo-Momma's, and other unworldly spirits. Ghosts meant serious trouble. Boo-Daddy's and Boo-Momma's would haunt you too. They were much the same, although Boo-Daddy's were of a mischievous nature and Boo-Momma's were less so.

A large winter garden full of turnips and collard greens grew near the house. I did not know who lived there, so I stopped on the road and remembered happy times. It was Catherine who taught me to cook and encouraged me when I was despondent over the death of my father. It would be easy to blame her for my weight gain through the years because anytime I cried she made cookies or a cake for me. But desserts weren't her only nurturing specialty. I still remember her putting a whole carrot in the middle of a pan of meat loaf so she could tell when it was done. In other words, when the fork went through the carrot easily, the meat loaf was ready to come out of the oven. That's how I cooked meat loaf too, until my husband introduced me to a meat thermometer. I recalled her hot corn bread and how enjoyable it was to pour pot liquor or sugar syrup over it as we ate it. Pot liquor is any liquid left in the pot after boiling vegetable greens. She was a skilled cook, and I wish I'd paid more attention to her cooking hints, but she was long gone, and her recipes gone with her.

Catherine taught us a song to sing before we ate and said grace.

If you sing at the table
And you whistle in the bed
The boggie-man will git you
Befo you be dead.

To this day, I have never sung at the table or whistled in the bed. My brother swears the same. This was one of the many admonitions delivered in childhood that stuck with us. Most of the others were of voodoo origins.

I drove a short distance and stopped. I was amazed at how small Jim and Zerelda's house was, but the old black wood stove was still there, even though everything else in the house was gone. The unpainted shack sat by the side of the road with all the windows now broken. A lone fragment of an Irish lace curtain at one window flapped with the breeze in and out of the opening. The house had three rooms – a kitchen, a living room, and a bedroom but no bathroom -- just an outhouse. It did have electricity: a single bulb hanging from a lone cord with a frayed pull hanging from the middle of the ceiling in each room.

Although the house personified stark poverty, my memories were of warm and loving times spent there. I closed my eyes and reminisced how Zerelda taught my brother and me how to suck the honeysuckle blooms which grew profusely behind the shack.

"Which one tastes best – the yellow or white one?" Zerelda always asked us. I was then and still am confused as to which nectar tasted best – that from the white bloom or the yellow bloom.

I also remember the delicious collard greens and cornbread hoe cakes she shared with us. Hoe cakes were cooked like pancakes on a hot griddle instead of baked in muffin tins in the oven. It was if I could still smell and taste those wonderful offerings from her wood stove in the kitchen.

Catherine always gave us a stern look when we told her how delicious the food was at Zerelda's house, but we knew she would sway us in her direction the next day.

"Now," she'd say, "how do you like my cooking today?"

We'd say, "You're the best cook in the world, Catherine." She'd smile and give us an extra dessert.

261

Next time we went to Zerelda's house we would repeat the process.

I looked out into the barren yard and recollected Zerelda's father George who couldn't read but could recite the Bible word for word all day. We were mesmerized by his holy knowledge as he sat, and sometimes stood, on an old stump and preached the gospel.

Jim, Zerelda's husband, worked every day. He'd hitch Old Pet up and plow all day. He never planted any seed.

My dad said, "Jim grows the best furrows in South Carolina." We'd laugh and then go tell Jim what Daddy said.

He would just beam and say, "That's why I work so hard. I wants to always do a good job."

I sometimes rode on the back of the plow horse and talk with him about his life. It was too late for his history because he didn't remember much of anything anymore.

He did remember the Yankees though. If he heard a car backfire, he'd yell, "Jump down, Missy. The Yankees must be nearby." We'd crouch as low as we could and listen for a while until he was satisfied the Yankees were gone.

My mother did have a small side garden, and Jim hoed the rows for her. It reminded him of his mother's garden.

"Where was your mother's garden, Jim," I remember my mother asking.

"Seems to me it was somewhere close by, but I don't remember where," he answered.

Years later when he passed away, we learned he was born in Edgefield County. That's as close as we ever came to knowing his origins other than he was born during the Civil War and was over one hundred years old when he passed away.

Our nanny, Jessie Bell Key, lived a mile away. She stayed in our house during the week and went home on Sunday for the day. She made sure we were clean and civil and spared us from many spankings. Some child, I don't remember who, told me she was a "nigger" when I first started school. I was surprised since I hadn't ever heard her called by that name before, so I came home and during my bath called her one. It was a bad decision on my part. She stood me up in the tub and spanked my bottom. I screamed, jumped out of the tub, and ran downstairs to tell my Daddy what had happened.

"That nigger just hit me," I said.

My daddy looked at the strangely and said, "What did you just say?

I repeated it and he took me firmly by the hand and paddled my bottom again.

"Don't use that word," he said. "It's not fitting for good people like Jessie Bell. Don't ever use it again." He pointed upstairs, and I crept back to the bathroom where Jessie Bell was waiting.

"I'm sorry," I said with tears in my eyes.

"I know you are, chile, just don't ever call me that again," she said.

The episode was never mentioned again. In those days the "n" word meant black trash, the same as white trash. That's the way I understood it.

Jessie Bell was college educated and also a practical nurse. She quit working in hospitals because the only job she was given was emptying bed pans. We were lucky to have her as a nanny.

I never visited her house but once that I can remember. It was well-furnished with a few Victorian antiques and lots of knick knacks. It had the faint aroma of something like incense, but I don't think it was a scent used in the church; it smelled sweeter and didn't make my eyes water. She was very religious and went to church every Sunday. Both of her parents had been teachers, and her father preached part time too.

The truth of Lily Twiggs' house stunned me. Hers was, at best, a destitute existence for her. It could only be labeled a shed and had two small rooms. The steps leading up to her front door, which I thought very steep and high as a child, were only three steps tall. As in Jim's cabin there was no insulation on the walls just bare wood. The old outhouse in the back was long gone. There was still no water and no electricity.

I must have worried about Lily's well-being when I was a child for, as I stood there, I recalled stealing canned goods from my mother's pantry and taking them to Lily. I don't remember why I kept quiet about taking the canned goods; there must have been a reason, but I don't remember it. I would hide them in a croaker sack and ride my pony over to her house to deliver the covert goods.

Alice Twiggs Vantrease

Lily was always appreciative and gracious and thin … painfully thin. Even though she was a very black woman, the blue veins were visible through her thin skin, and her hands shook.

She ironed everything we used. When my mother noticed it was becoming hard for her to iron the sheets because of her age, she bought her a pressing board which allowed her to iron large portions of the sheets at one time, and she could sit in a chair while she worked too. She always hummed a sad little tune while she ironed. I couldn't understand the words, and the cook Catherine said she was singing in an African language.

One day I said, "Lily, what do the words to the song mean?"

"I don't know, Missy," she said, "My momma always sang it to the babies when they was little, and I reckon her momma sang it too."

"You never asked her what they meant?"

"NO, Missy. We was too busy doing chores once we was old enough to move around."

I vaguely remember the tune to the song, but nothing about the African words. I wish I had been old enough to write them down phonetically.

I sat down on Lily's front steps and reminded myself that perspective changes as we grow taller and older. What had not changed were the happy memories of my time spent with these individuals as a child. Nevertheless, my heart ached when I thought of the hardships endured right under my nose without my having had any sense of the misery..

Even though I rationally realize there was nothing I could have done as a child to change anything in the lives of these loved ones, I can't shake the mantle of guilt I now carry. Some white children were also marked by the societal remnants of slavery … and I am one of them.

I wish I had been able to make in a difference in their lives because their kindness certainly made a difference in mine. I am who I am today in part due to their nurturing, and I wouldn't change it for anything on earth.

.

Excerpt from Mrs. Bull

Mrs. Bull

Mrs. Laura Lee Bull lived on the other side of us but was almost never home. Her twin sister, Miss Sadie Mae Phinizy, lived just down the street. Miss Sadie Mae had never married and before she started losing her memory, she would substitute at bridge when one of the other players couldn't make the game.

Mrs. Bull didn't come home to Summerville very often. She was working in Washington, DC, where she was secretary to a large environmental association and active in the Democratic Party. "Tree huggers and squirrel kissers," Gram said about anyone who was a Democrat.

Gram also said Mrs. Bull had one daughter who lived clear across the country in California. "Her daughter Phyllis couldn't have moved any further away from her mother and still be in the United States unless she relocated to Alaska."

That was Gram's way of saying Mrs. Bull and her daughter didn't get along. She said Miss Phyllis was a skunk of a lawyer and had six children. "Phyllis is just like her mother, except she is reproducing like a rat." My grandmother didn't think much of Mrs. Bull's daughter. The day would come when I didn't think much of her either.

I did like Mrs. Bull's sister. Miss Sadie Mae came by Mrs. Bull's house every day to check on things and to ask Grover, the caretaker, what he was doing there. Grover, like our maid Beulah, said Miss Sadie Mae was getting "old timer's" disease and couldn't remember a thing, but he told her he was the caretaker just the same. He told her the same thing every day, and Miss Sadie May would come right back the next day to repeat the conversation. I never tired of meeting her for the first time.

Listening to Miss Sadie Mae drove Beulah crazy because when she was in our kitchen, she could hear everything that was said next door when Miss Sadie Mae came by to ask about her sister. "Why don't he tell her she's gone somewhere forever and put us all out of our misery?" Beulah said one day.

Gram answered, "Nobody's ever gone forever if they leave some good behind them. Sadie Mae Phinizy has done a lot of good on this earth." My grandmother subscribed to the philosophy that old people should be given lots of patience. Beulah clearly didn't have patience and continued to be agitated over the situation. She was particularly stressed when no one was home next door and Sadie Mae came over to our house looking for her missing sister. Beulah finally made a sign and put it on the outside of the door. It said "Mrs. Bull is not home. She is in Washington, DC." That solved the problem for a while. Sadie Mae was forgetful, but she could still read.

Mrs. Bull belonged to the National Organization of Women (NOW,) but she didn't admit it to anyone. I discovered her membership card in an old alligator handbag after she'd thrown it away. It is a mystery to me now as to why I wanted it, but I snatched it from the top of her waste can before the garbage truck came by. The bag intrigued me and seemed like the perfect case to stash secret papers in. It was kept it in the top of my closet where I knew no one would look.

When I finally told my grandmother about Mrs. Bull's NOW membership,, she said, "Well, it's no surprise to me. Laura Lee's ugly as sin. You might know she'd join that type of organization. She shaves her upper lip too. It would look better waxed." She admonished me to never let anyone know I was foraging in trash cans looking for stuff to stow away in my bedroom.

"I can't imagine anyone not being liberated," she'd said every time the subject came up. "All a woman has to do is turn off the loving, and a man'll give her anything she wants." And God forbid anyone should mention the National Organization of Women. "Look at them," she'd say. "What a spectacle. Ugly. The whole lot of them. They're just plain ugly. Why they don't even wax the dark hairs on their upper lips. No wonder they don't have a man around. Men don't like to kiss a woman with a mustache."

I tried countless times to argue that many of the members of NOW were beautiful and very educated, but she wouldn't hear of it. "They're ugly," she'd say, "and stupid too."

Women can be mean at times, and my grandmother was no exception. She shared the newfound knowledge about Mrs. Bull's membership in NOW at the next bridge club meeting, and half the time was spent arguing the pro's and con's of being an uppity woman. Miss Myrtis said acting smart never got a woman anywhere. All the others disagreed with her and said being uppity was the best way to keep a man. "Treat them like hell, and they'll keep coming back for more; Be nice to them, and they'll go find a mistress who'll treat them like hell," they said.

When I told Grover about the conversation he just shook his head and said, "Some things never change. Most women are born mean and just get meaner after that."

Mrs. Bull developed cancer soon after, and her daughter moved her to the West Coast against her will. A short time later we heard that she had passed away.

It's hard to recapture the absurdity of those days when Sallie Mae was looking for her sister all the time and grieving anew whenever she was told Mrs. Bull was dead.

"Oh, no," she'd say. "Laura Lee's dead? Oh I can't believe it. My sister's dead." Then she'd burst into tears and moan from the depths of her soul until someone heard her, changed the subject, and shepherded her back home.

Finally, when Laura Lee had been dead for over a month, Beulah had had enough. When Sallie Mae arrived the next day and asked Mrs. Bull's maid about her sister, Beulah yelled out, "For God's sake, tell her Laura Lee's on a trip to Paris. Tell her anything. Quit making her grieve anew each day. She won't remember anything tomorrow anyhow. Don't tell her Laura Lee's dead anymore."

Unfortunately, Beulah yelled so loud Sadie Mae heard her. "Laura Lee's dead? She's dead? I can't believe it. Laura Lee's dead." She was sobbing out loud and lifting her arms up to the sky. "I can't believe it. Laura Lee's dead." She kept up the refrain until her nurse changed the subject and she forgot Laura Lee was dead again.

That's the last time we had to listen to Sadie Mae grieve for her sister. From then on, everyone just lied through their teeth and told how Mrs. Bull was traveling the world and going to all sorts of exotic places. Every now and then Grover would say Mrs. Bull was in Morocco or Afghanistan studying to become a Muslim. This really stirred things up and Sadie Mae would head off to St. Anne's to tell the priest Laura Bell was a heretic.

When she couldn't remember why she was at church, the priest would tell her how lovely she looked. The compliment lifted her spirits and quickened her step. Sadie Mae glided along the sidewalk until she reached home and forgot all about it again.

We kept up the charade for almost a full year until Sadie Mae passed away. During that time she marveled at all the places her sister was traveling. Beulah said it was a good thing Sadie Mae was finally gone because we had run out of places for Mrs. Bull to go without repeating a trip.

Sadie Mae had a small graveside funeral, but we were all there. There wasn't a dry eye in the house when the service ended.

About the Author

Alice Twiggs Vantrease grew up in South Carolina and spent her summers with her Grandmother Wright in the South Carolina Lowcountry. Following a normal liberal arts education, she received a degree in Confusion from the Institute of Marriage where major areas of interest were concentrated in diaper changing and cheese grits. She received an advanced degree in the School of Media Obfuscation where her thesis "The Importance of Truth in News Reporting" was solidly rejected. Final thesis topic was "Rejection: Why Salespeople Love Sales." She is currently pursuing a Ph.D. in the School of Dirty Knees where her thesis "Advice to a New Gardener from a Used One" is under current review.

Alice claims to be a truly liberated woman: Her children are grown and the dog is finally housebroken. Now taking a sabbatical from the media and marketing rat race, she is pursuing her interest in writing, painting, and needlework. In addition to *The Rabbit in the Moon – A Garden Tale for the Young and the Young at Heart*, she is the author of *Charlie's Secret,* a novel set in the Lowcountry of South Carolina.

The Hootchie Cootchie Pickler and Other Southern Tales is her first book of short stories. When she isn't painting needlepoint canvases, she continues to write.

Alice has appeared on the *Tales From the South* radio program on Arkansas Public Radio where she read one of her short stories, *Strom Thurmond's Tea Party (Not to be confused with today's political party as the story takes place in 1948*.) A podcast of that program can be found on the NPR web site. She has been invited to appear there again in the near future with a reading of another of her short stories *The Messin' Potion* which appears in this book.

Alice now resides in North Carolina but visits Savannah on a regular basis to attend meetings of the *Savannah Authors* writing group. She is currently working on *The Second Coming of Mrs. Bull,* a collection of short stories set in Augusta, Ga.

The Hootchie Cootchie Pickler
and Other Southern Tales

Additional information: *Tales from the South* is a weekly NPR show that features Southerners reading their own true stories in front of a live audience during dinner at various locally-owned restaurants and other venues throughout Arkansas. Home station is the University of Arkansas at Little Rock's KUAR, and *Tales* is heard on multiple public radio stations across the country and satellite radio around the world. The show is distributed by Public Radio Exchange (PRX) to multiple public radio stations throughout the country. It is also syndicated by World Radio Network (WRN) and is heard six times a week on WRN Europe, WRN Asia, and WRN Africa; twice a week on RTE, Ireland's Public Broadcasting Service; once a week on Poland's Public Radio; and once a week on World Radio Paris, the only broadcast licensed to broadcast in English in Paris. Podcasts are available on Stitcher Smart Radio, the NPR website, the KUAR website, the PRX website, and the *Tales from the South* website. In 2012 the program won PRX's Zeitfunk Award for Most Licensed Debut Producer, and in 2013 it won a Governors' Arts Award, was in the top six

281

storytelling shows on Stitcher Smart Radio (with *This American Life, StoryCorps, The Moth, Risk!* and *Snap Judgment*), and won a 2014 Henry Award through Arkansas Parks and Tourism. In June 2014 *Tales from the South* was included in *The Encyclopedia of Arkansas History and Culture*. *Tales* recently partnered with *Snap Judgment* and stories are now heard there, too. *Tales* is on the Arkansas Arts Council's Arts on Tour Roster and is presented by William F. Laman Public Library, with additional support provided by the *Oxford American Magazine*, the Writers' Colony at Dairy Hollow, *AY Magazine,* UALR's Department of Rhetoric and Writing, and the North Little Rock Visitors' Bureau. Live shows are at multiple restaurants and venues throughout Central Arkansas and the rest of the state.

Books by Alice Twiggs Vantrease:

The Hootchie Cootchie Pickler
and Other Southern Tales

The Rabbit in the Moon: A Garden Tale for the Young and
the Young at Heart

Charlie's Secret

Available Soon:

The Second Coming of Mrs. Bull

18747845R00169

Made in the USA
Middletown, DE
19 March 2015